For the laidback
Mr Gumjoy

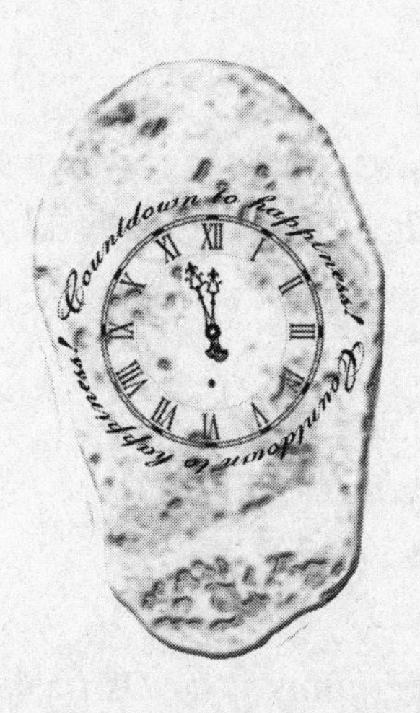

I crouch down on the pavement . . . and gasp.

I'm looking at a perfect, dainty clock face, painted on to an imperfect circle of dried-up old chewing gum.

The smaller of the feathery black hands is pointing to twelve, while the longer one is just about to catch up with it.

Around the edge of the clock face, there's some spidery, swirly writing.

It reads: Countdown to happiness!

Shivers of shock ripple through me.

(It's good that I'm kneeling down, otherwise I might just fall over.)

So . . . the happiness clock is real.

Tiny.

Made of gum.

But real.

And there I was, thinking it was just some nuts idea that existed in the privacy of my head.

(The blood pounds in my ears like a demented tick-tock.)

Why have I found this?

What is it trying to tell me?

Is it some kind of clue?

A message?

Wouldn't it be funny if it was trying to let me know that it was time for my stupid, spiky life to change. . .?

Chapter 1

Ten Things I Hate

1. People who argue.
Especially parents.

2. People arguing who say they aren't.
They come out with stuff like, "But Edie, we're not *really* arguing! We're just . . . *discussing* things!" Yeah, like everyone enjoys "discussing things" in loud voices, while throwing mugs at each other's heads.

3. Nits.
The only specialist hair product a girl my age (thirteen) should have is a super-shine serum. Me? I have super-strength nit shampoo, thanks to having a six-year-old brother called Stan whose school seems to double as a petting zoo for head lice.

4. Grown girls with teddies on their beds.
What's that all about? Soft toys are for little kids, like Stan. My best friend, Tash, has one of those sad-looking, grey furry bears that are meant to melt your heart. It makes me want to get a pair of scissors and go into a slashing frenzy.

5. Films with happy endings you can see coming a mile off.
Mum loves making me watch them with her once Stan's gone to bed. As the kiss is about to happen for the man and woman who've spent the last hour and a half huffing with each other, my mum will be crying and *I* will be trying not to vomit at the cutesiness of it all.

6. False nails.
They creep me out. A bunch of sixth-form girls wear them at school and think they look beyond excellent. And I guess they *are* beyond excellent, if you're into having something that looks like alien lobster claws. Our fourth or fifth nanny had them too. She'd drum those weird square nails on the granite kitchen worktop whenever she wanted to kill me.

7. Sleeping on the top bunk.

It gives me vertigo, it really does. That's so lame, isn't it? I offered Stan a month's pocket money or a new Star Wars Lego set to swap, but he said no. Then I offered him a month's pocket money AND a new Star Wars Lego set and he STILL said no. At least I've only got to do it at Dad's place.

At Mum's, I've got to put up with the stupid old clock in the hall that Nana gave to us when she downsized and moved into her bungalow. I used to quite like it when it sat on her glass china cabinet. I hate it now, 'cause I lie awake in middle of the night, listening to its loud tick-tock, marking off the minutes like some ominous clock of *doom*.

8. Yellow.

Too ridiculously cheerful for its own good. The colour Mum painted my room without asking, just after she split with Dad. I think it was meant to lift my spirits. As if I'd be so wowed by the daffodilly shade that I might not notice Dad wasn't living with us any more.

9. Cheese.

Especially when it's melted. Though I guess it's fine if you like eating something that tastes like warm, orange elastic bands. I've lost count of the nannies who've flipped out 'cause I've said no to pizza. "But *every* kid loves pizza!" they say. "Not THIS kid. . ." I'll mumble, while I shove my plate away and stick my nose back in my book.

10. BFPs.

"I do not, repeat do *not*, need a nanny!" I told Mum, when she dropped the bombshell about *paying* people to pick up me and Stan from school.

I really resent the fact that Mum (*and* Dad) don't trust me to look after *myself*, never mind Stan.

And I *loathe* the word "nanny", though it's better than "babysitter" or "childminder", since I'm not a baby *or* a child, obviously.

What I *have* been since Mum and Dad split up is one very angry teenager.

An angry teenager who can spot a BFP (Big Fat Phoney) a mile off. The nannies; the stupidly *huge* amount of nannies we've ended up having: every single one of them has been a BFP. They've all pretended they like children. Or at least pretended to Mum and Dad that they like me and Stan.

Of course they don't, as me and Stan like to prove,

what with our gentle torturing and intimidation and everything. . .

But hey, nobody wants to hear me moaning and grouching about things I hate, do they?

Specially Mum and Dad, who're *very* busy people.

Busy with their hectic work schedules and sniping at each other.

So I'll keep the moaning and grouching to myself.

Or offload a little to my best friend Tash.

Or better still, go to the top of the nearest mountain and YELL my worries into the wind!

Pity I live in the centre of a city without a mountain in sight.

OK, so let's add one *more* thing to my "Things I Hate" list. . .

11. Not getting what I want.

Like handy local mountains, parents who like each other and a family that's vaguely happy.

But, hey, I guess it's asking too much to expect that stuff.

Right?

"Right," sighs the world, with a shrug of its shoulders. . .

Chapter 2

Life As We Know It

If only, if only, if only. . .

If only it was just me and Stan at home.

4.30 p.m.: I could leave my after-school club early.

4.45 p.m.: I could pick up my little brother from his.

By 5 p.m., I could be lying on the sofa reading, with Radio One burbling in the background and a huge bag of nachos by my side.

Stan could be scuttling about on his bedroom floor, constructing his latest Lego mega-structure while popping M&M's.

Instead, we're trapped here with a large woman called Miranda who insists on . . .

a) cooking us a variation of the same terrible tea every night (burnt burgers and chips, burnt burgers and rice, burnt burgers and pasta. . .)

b) having the TV tuned into stupid shopping channels the whole time, and . . .

c) chatting about the offers they have on there (like me and Stan are remotely interested in state-of-the-art electric tin openers and tummy-trimming granny pants).

Miranda is the latest in a long, *long* line of nannies who've looked after me and my brother while Mum works.

That's if we're staying at Mum's.

If we're staying at Dad's, we get picked up from school by Cheryl. Cheryl is addicted to chewing gum and texting, which sounds a lot quieter than Miranda's shopping channels, but the constant *sneck, sneck, sneck* of chewing and tapping can send you *mad*.

A few hours of looking after/ignoring/irritating us later, Miranda (or Cheryl or whoever) will do the Big Fat Phoney routine, smiling sweetly at Mum or Dad as they come in the door, patting Stan on the head like he's some kind of dog and pretending it's been a total delight to spend time with us.

Yeah, *right*.

Though try getting Mum or Dad to see that. They'd rather believe a brain-dead gum-chewer or a shopping channel addict than us.

And this, ladies and gentlemen, boys and girls, is life as we know it for me and Stan.

How tragic is that?

"Edie . . . you're *scratching* again!"

Miranda's voice booms like a foghorn across the room. She could say, "Edie, you've won a year's supply of cash and nachos!" and I'd still be grinding my teeth at the very sound of all that booming.

If she turned down the telly for once, maybe she'd be able to speak at a normal volume. But the TV roars away, only getting switched off a couple of minutes before Mum is due back. That way, she walks into a flat that seems to be some calm oasis of well-fed kids, quietly doing their homework. (Phoney, phoney, phoney. . .)

"We have some little visitors *again*, do we?" Miranda nags on.

"Little visitors?" I repeat, pretending I haven't a clue what she means.

"*Nits*, Edie!" Miranda spells out. "Have you got nits again? I saw you scratching just now. . ."

"I wasn't scratching. I was running my fingers through my hair," I tell her.

I try running my fingers through my hair now, in the hope that it'll make my lie seem true. But I can see from the reflection in the computer screen that it's not looking too convincing; I'm wincing at the knots at the back. I've taken to brushing just the top of my hair and hoping no one spots the matted bits I can't be bothered to sort out underneath.

"Hmmm. . ." I hear Miranda mutter, as she bustles off to the kitchen to scrub the burnt frying pan.

"You *were* scratching," Stan comes and whispers in my ear.

The reflection of his freckly face is right beside mine on the computer screen. With our little and large heads together like this, it makes a handy bridge for all his brand new nits to wander across into the exciting new territory of my hair, where they can hook up with the current batch who are driving me INSANE.

"Edie!" shrills Miranda, reappearing in the doorway. "You hardly ate any of your tea!"

She says this while holding out my untouched plate and staring at the woman on the telly demonstrating all the ways you can wear this season's on-trend snood.

"Did you know," I begin, ignoring Miranda's statement, "that seventy-three per cent of people who order from shopping channels get themselves into debt, buying stuff they don't need?"

"Oh!" gasps Miranda, sounding worried. "Is that a fact?"

"Yes."

No, it isn't.

I just made it up.

I enjoy unnerving nannies with random, untrue facts. And because I'm always either on the computer or reading, they seem to believe me. The fools.

"What does 'in debt' mean?" asks Stan.

"People spending money they don't have," I explain.

"Oh. Are you in debt?" Stan asks Miranda.

"Yes, *are* you?" I add bluntly.

Miranda is all red-cheeked and flustered. Adults can't stand talking about money. It's like asking them to show you their knickers. But I am very good at asking embarrassing questions with a straight face, and making nannies squirm.

The trick is to act very serious, so they can't accuse you of being cheeky.

It's excellent fun.

"Well . . . I . . . I mean, no!" Miranda flusters. "And anyway, it's not really any of your business!"

"Sorry," I apologize, straight-faced. "I didn't mean to upset you. You're right; if you're having money troubles, it really isn't any of our business. . ."

"I don't have 'money troubles', Edie! And if I did, I'd hardly be telling *you*!" says Miranda, stomping back into the kitchen.

Great. I've got her fizzing. Now to go in for the kill.

I look around and spot Stan's empty glass of milk. I pick it up and take it through to the kitchen, pretending I'm just being terribly helpful.

Stan – my ever-willing accomplice – trots after me.

"You know, if you're worried about money, perhaps you should think about getting a better paid job, Miranda," I suggest, putting the glass in the dishwasher.

"I'm NOT worried about money, Edie *dear*!" she says snippily, scraping the cremated burger and beans into the bin.

"Doesn't Mummy pay you very much?" Stan asks Miranda, tilting his head to the side and staring up with innocent six-year-old eyes.

"Now, it's not polite to ask how much people earn, Stanley!" Miranda tells him, clattering the plate into the sink so hard I think it might have cracked.

"Especially when people are having money troubles, Stan," I add.

"Edie! I do NOT have money troubles!" snaps Miranda, now picking up the blackened frying pan from the cooker hob. "How many times do I have to say it?!"

She is one step away from losing it, I'm sure. Just one more little push. . .

"Sorry. I know when people are worried about money it can very stressful."

"FOR THE LAST TIME!" Miranda shouts at me. "WILL YOU SHUT UP ABOUT—"

She stops dead and stares at Mum, who's standing in the kitchen doorway with her keys in her hand and a "Surprise! I'm home early!" expression on her face fading into something altogether darker.

Perfecto!

Couldn't have timed that better myself.

I mean. . .

- TV blaring? (Check.)
- Scarlet-faced nanny yelling at me and Stan? (Check.)
- Scarlet-faced nanny brandishing a frying pan? (Check.)

Miranda is *history*.

"That's it!" grunts Miranda. "No more! I've had enough of these children, Mrs Henderson. You can keep your job!"

Mum says nothing – just holds out her hand for the spare keys, like she's done so many times before.

With much huffing and puffing, Miranda grabs her jacket and bag, rifles for the keys in her pocket, hands them to Mum, then bumbles out into the hall without a backwards glance but with a dramatic slam of the door.

"*What* happened there?" asks Mum, walking over to the TV and switching it off, just as the phoney presenter holds up the tackiest, ugliest piece of jewellery I've ever seen and describes it as "exquisite".

"You didn't believe us, Mum!" I begin. "But that's what she's always like – she just sits watching the shopping channels or else she's shouting at us!"

That was half a lie and half a truth, so I don't feel *too* terrible.

Especially if it means we're one step closer to our number one wish: me and Stan, to be left *alone*. . .

"Well, she might not have been perfect," sighed Mum. "But what am I going to do now?"

"Listen, *I* can pick up Stan from his after-school club and look after him here!" I offer, for the four hundredth time. (One of these days, Mum's going to crack and say "OK", I hope.)

"But Edie, you're only just thirteen!" Mum tells me, as if I didn't know it. "You have homework to concentrate on, and friends to see after school sometimes. What happens if you want to go round to Tash's?"

"Stan can come with me! Tash likes Stan."

"I can be quiet! I could just take some Lego with me!" Stan chips in.

But Mum's not listening to us. She's flopped herself up against the sink and has her head in her hands. She's done that a lot in the last few months.

"Hey, what's up?" comes Dad's voice.

Mum's head snaps up.

"What are you doing here, Neil?" she asks, all bristly.

"I'm just on my way to a meeting. Stan left his PE kit at mine last night, so I thought I'd better drop it off on the way," he answers, holding up a blue nylon bag. "And as tomorrow's Thursday, he'll need it, won't you, tiger?"

Dad ruffles Stan's hair, and Stan growls happily on cue.

"How did you get in here, Neil?" she asks.

Mum now sounds growly, but not in a fun way.

"With these, of course!" he laughs, holding up his set of flat keys, the ones with the "World's Best Dad" motto dangling from them.

Mum is staring at him as if he is the world's worst soon-to-be ex-husband.

"Neil – they are for *emergencies*. You can't come and go as you like. It's not your home any more!"

Our flat hasn't been Dad's home for three and a half months (and four days, if you want to get technical). Not since the night Mum threw his favourite Arsenal mug at his head (there's still a dent where it hit – the wall, not his head, thank goodness).

He went to live with his mate Eric after that, till he got his flat in that new block overlooking the canal. That's where we stay every Tuesday and

Friday night now, plus all day Saturday. Dad tells people that this is his "quality time" with us, which is a good description, I guess, if you think watching your dad working on his computer while you catalogue strange things floating in the canal counts as "quality time".

Mum fibs quite a lot as well – she tells everyone that the split is "amicable". In most dictionaries, "amicable" means "friendly". But Mum obviously uses a *different* dictionary, one where "amicable" means "horrible".

"OK, Justine, message understood," says Dad, holding his hands up in surrender. "From now on, I will ring the doorbell. Or maybe phone first, to see if I have your *permission* to ring the doorbell. Or would you like me to get *my* solicitor to get in touch with *your* solicitor, to see if it's all right for me to return Stan's sports bag?"

"There's no need for that, Neil!" Mum says sharply.

Right, time for me and Stan to go. Listening to your parents having hissy fits with each other is about as much of a laugh as getting sand kicked in your eyes.

"Come on," I say to Stan, pulling him by the

sleeve of his school shirt. "Let's leave Mum and Dad to enjoy their argument. . ."

"We're not *arguing*, Edie!" they burst out at the same time, then get flustered with shock at agreeing on something for once. Even if it happens to be a lie.

"Whoops – silly me for thinking that you were!" I say sarcastically.

Stan nuzzles into my side. He goes pretty silent at times like these.

"Your dad and I get on fine," Mum announces. "Don't we, Neil?"

"Yes, of course!" Dad replies, through gritted teeth.

Wow, how lousy is it when your own parents are world-class BFPs?

"In fact, Neil – I'm glad you're here," Mum carries on, widening her mouth in what I think is supposed to look like a smile. "I just found out that I have to go away for a work conference on the Saturday after next, to plan the new design range. I won't be back till late, so would you be all right to have Edie and Stan stay for two nights instead of one?"

"Well . . . *no*, actually," Dad answers bluntly. "I was going to ask *you* to have the kids that Saturday! I've got a really important meeting with a new client then. It's out of town, so I might have to stay over and—"

Mum's fake smile flicks off. "And when were you planning to tell me about this?"

Uh-oh, here we go again. I nudge Stan and, arms around each other, we take a few backwards steps, like we're doing a three-legged race in reverse.

"I only just had it confirmed ten minutes ago!" Dad says defensively, brandishing his BlackBerry. "You're not the *only* one with a career, you know, Justine!"

"Yeah, a career I can't do properly because you keep letting me down, and now Miranda has just walked out and—"

"Well, it's hardly *my* fault if—"

CLUNK!

I shut the kitchen door and shut out the sniping.

"Stress snack?" I suggest to Stan.

"Mmm," he mumbles, looking up at me with his Malteser eyes.

We head off to my room, where we'll raid the box under the bed that I keep my stash of KitKats, Rolos and other assorted yumminess in. There's a handwritten note taped to the top of the box that says: "EDIE AND STAN'S EMRGIZEE CHOCLIT –

HANDS OF!" (Hopefully, you'll have a pretty good idea which one of us wrote that.)

I came up with the idea of stress snacks when our parents gave up on saving their arguments till after Stan went to bed.

It was obviously around the time I gave up on trying to pretend to my little brother that everything was OK with our family.

Speaking of time, as we slouch off towards my room and the awaiting emergency chocolate (Snickers for me, Mars Bar for Stan) the antique clock of doom on the hall table chimes to let us know it's quarter past five.

With every dull, slightly out-of-tune chime that old clock makes, my heart sinks.

It arrived when my parents started fighting more, and it's like a permanent reminder (*tick-tock, tick-tock*) that there's something wrong, all wrong, with our family.

You know, sometimes I feel like picking it up and chucking it out of the window. How great would it feel to see it smashed to pieces and silent on the pavement?

Then me and Stan could go shopping for a *new* clock. One that's bright, shiny white instead of old, dark wood. One that tinkles prettily on the hour, making a sound that almost gets you giggling.

A clock that makes you excited about what's coming next, instead of dreading it.

Yep, that's what me and Stan need: a happiness clock.

But what's the point of wishing for things that don't exist or will never happen?

It's better not to think about the future.

All I can do is try and make the here and now OK for Stan.

"D'you want my Snickers bar too?" I whisper to my brother, as I push my bedroom door open.

"Yay!" Stan yells in a whisper back.

"One condition," I add. "Just don't be sick afterwards. . ."

See? I am *such* a caring sister.

Chapter 3

Me and Stan Against the World

Tash is in love.

"Check this out!" she says, holding up her phone for me to see.

"Wow, it's twenty-five to four!" I say sarcastically, as I stare at the time digitally displayed on her screen.

"Oops – not that. *This!*" she giggles, swiping and pressing before presenting the phone to me again.

It's her latest photos of Max.

Max at the beach, Max sitting on the steps by the churchyard, Max lounging on Tash's bed, Max bent over and licking his. . .

"Ugh! That is disgusting!" I say, wincing.

Max might be one very cute puppy, but this particular pose isn't exactly picturesque.

"Oh, I meant to delete that one," says Tash, pressing a button on her phone.

"You'll be taking pictures of him pooing in the park next!" I grumble as we stroll out of the annexe where the after-school club is held.

I'm strolling because I'm in no rush to meet whoever will be picking me up at the school gate. It'll be just another agency nanny, someone Mum will have sorted out at short notice to replace Miranda, and had to pay a fortune for the privilege. This stranger will have collected Stan from his primary school down the road, and will be holding his hand, without caring or knowing anything about him. The fact that his favourite Smarties are the blue ones and that he wants to be either a Lego designer or a crocodile when he grows up would probably disinterest her no end.

"Edie! What's *wrong* with you today?" Tash suddenly bursts in. "You're in a *really* rubbish mood!"

Tash is my best friend, and I feel sorry for her sometimes. Being my best friend must be *really* hard work. I mean, I've always been kind of sarcastic, while she's quite sunshiney. But I think the last few months I've become ever more gloomy and I'm worried she might have run out of rays of sunshine while trying to brighten me up.

And she's right (of course). I *am* in a more-rubbish-than-usual mood today. Part of it is 'cause it was zero fun seeing Mum and Dad grouching with each other last night. At least with them living apart, me and Stan normally just have to put up with them being all stiff and distant when they're dropping us off between flats. I lay awake for ages last night, running over the sniping again and again, while the clock of doom ominously clacked the after-midnight hours away.

Another reason for the more-rubbish-than-usual mood is that my head has been maddeningly itchy, as the old nits appear to have been partying with the new nits. (Not for much longer; I'm going to spend my allowance on nuclear-strength head-lice shampoo later, since Mum keeps forgetting to buy any.)

Yet *another* reason is because I just heard the biggest, fattest, *phoniest* line ever this afternoon.

"*Just believe in your dreams, and they really will come true!*"

How phoney is that?

You've heard it before, I'm sure; celebs always like to trot that out in their cheesy magazine interviews. The trouble is, it's easy to say when you're wildly successful, isn't it? But out of one hundred per cent of people holding tight to some kind of precious dream, you can bet that less than .0000001 per cent will *ever* have their dreams come true.

Yes, I made that fact up, but I'm pretty sure I believe it.

"I didn't like that woman today. She got on my nerves," I tell Tash, as I try to explain myself.

"Yeah? But you love her books!"

We're talking about this author of vampire novels who'd come to do a talk at our school for Book Week. I'm not going to say her name, 'cause that'll just give her free publicity, and she doesn't deserve any. I mean, she talked about her latest book and how she wrote it, which was interesting and brilliant and everything. Then it got to the bit where we could ask questions, and Charlotte Adamson stuck her hand up and said, "*I've* got an idea for a book. Do you think it'll get published one day?"

And the author-who-I-won't-name said; "Well, if you just believe in your dreams, they *will* come true!"

Blam.

That's when I went from total fan to complete ex-fan.

At the same time, Charlotte Adamson was suddenly all flustery with excitement, already planning her outfit for the Book Of The Year Awards and thinking what type of luxury flat she'd buy with all the money she's going to make from her bestseller.

But what everyone except the author-who-I-won't-name knows is that Charlotte Adamson has all the writing ability of a brick and her book idea is so bad it *hurts*.

Next thing, the author-who-I-won't-name turned away from Charlotte Adamson and asked if there were any other questions.

Big mistake.

As you may have spotted, I am *excellent* at hitting people with questions they aren't going to like.

So up went my hand and I said, "Charlotte's book idea; it's about a goat."

"A goat with magic eyes!" Charlotte Adamson chipped in, all smiles.

"So," I carried on, "do you think you could help her get it published?"

Mr Newsome, the teacher, had to step in at that point, because the author-who-I-won't-name was wriggling uncomfortably. She could now see that it didn't matter *how* much Charlotte dreamt the dream, a novel about a magic-eyed goat just isn't going to get book publishers rushing to pay her JK Rowling-style squillions.

"She was a complete BFP," I tell Tash, as I start to scan the small huddle of waiting adults at the gates, some with little brothers and sisters and dogs in tow. They're the ones who live far enough away to drive their kids home. Everyone else walks home alone. Everyone except me, since my mum seems to be under the illusion that I am in fact five years old, and not a teenager at secondary school.

"That woman didn't like it when she realized what she'd written in your book," says Tash, sticking her phone in her bag.

You bet she didn't. The author-who-I-won't-name was signing books afterwards, and I'd already bought my copy in advance (before I realized she was a BFP). She swirled her fancy signature and then asked what *my* name was.

"Ellie. . ." I lied, watching her purple pen scribble on the title page, "Phant. That's P-H-A-N-T."

She'd frowned up at me, wondering why I'd want to take the mickey out of her and deface my own book at the same time.

I didn't waste an explanation on her, but if I'd wanted to, I'd have said I just fancied messing with her mind, the way *she'd* messed with Charlotte Adamson's.

And if there hadn't been a queue of my classmates waiting to get their books signed (with their real names inside) I'd've taken out my phone and shown her a photo of Stan, in all his smiling, freckled glory. I'd've said, "See this kid? *His* dream is that our mum and dad will get back together. And no matter how much he believes it, trust me, it's *not* going to happen. So if someone like you goes around getting people's hopes up about stuff, well, it's basically plain *cruel*."

"Hey, Edie – there's Stan," I heard Tash say in a strangely confused way. "But he doesn't look like he's with anyone!"

I stare where she's staring.

Sure enough, the straggle of adults by the big metal gate are all familiar faces, come to collect their kids and ferry them home in a selection of cars, all parked along the tree-lined street. But there is no *unknown* face there; no agency stranger holding my little brother's hand.

"Stan!" I call over, and he waves at me brightly.

His new school blazer is way too big for him and he looks comically small standing there on his own.

In a few rushed seconds we're with him, and he is looking very pleased with himself.

"I walked here all on my own, Edie!" he beams. "I was *ever* so very careful crossing the road!"

"But *why* are you on your own? Didn't you get picked up?" asks Tash.

"Nobody came!" he says simply.

"But your teachers – what did they say? And why did they let you go?" I ask, knowing how strict his school is about kids and their safety.

"I think Miss Stewart went to the office to see if anyone called. And Miss Jessop was at the gate, but then Cody fell off the monkey bars and was screaming and when Miss Jessop went to see if he'd broken anything I pretended I'd seen you and just left."

"You shouldn't have done that, Stan!" I tell him, cross with worry.

But at the same time, I feel a little flurry of excitement.

So maybe the agency mucked up; so maybe this is the perfect opportunity to prove something to Mum. . .

*

Most of the time it feels as if it's me and Stan against the world, but now and then it's like the world owes us a break.

It's five p.m., according to the chiming clock of doom in the hall, and I am lying on the sofa reading, with Radio One burbling in the background and a huge bag of nachos by my side.

Stan is scuttling about on his bedroom floor, constructing his latest Lego mega-structure while popping M&M's.

There is pasta boiling in the kitchen, and broccoli too, and I have grated some cheese for Stan, even though cheese is evil and me and it do NOT get along.

Oh, yes, everything is under control and Mum is going to be super impressed. She is going to see that me and Stan are absolutely fine on our own, and she will never again feel the need to inflict an unwanted nanny on us.

She will then tell Dad that we can be home alone, no problemo, and he can sack gum-chewing Cheryl – by text, probably, since that's the only way she communicates.

It's going to be great!

Ding dong!

Who's that? Mum without her keys? Maybe. Her work bag is this giant, sloppy, tan leather sack thing that she loves 'cause she can fit in her work laptop, a pair of flat shoes and her packed lunch. In amongst that lot, her keys often take about a year to find.

I jump up off the sofa and abandon my book in the muddle of squashy sofa cushions.

"Is that Mum?" asks Stan, joining me in the hall. He's carrying a complex-looking Lego structure that's probably meant to be a space shuttle or something I guess I should recognize.

"I suppose so," I tell him, as I go to grab the door latch. "Though she's a bit early. . ."

Since the company she works for promoted her to head designer last year, Mum has never been home before seven p.m., and if there's a deadline happening, she can be out till *way* past Stan's bedtime. It's always extra lousy then. Just me and some random nanny on our own. Imagine the thrills and excitement of back-to-back soaps on telly (snore. . .).

"Mum, wait till you see my Lego armadillo!" Stan calls out, ever hopeful.

And prepare to be amazed and impressed by how

capable we are, Mum! I think to myself, with a sideways glance at Stan's unidentifiable work of Lego art.

"It's only me, Edith!" says Mrs Kosma.

Mrs Kosma is our older-than-old neighbour from downstairs. She is very small (about up to my nose) and very wide. She has an amazing selection of (wide) black dresses. When they are hanging on the washing line in the communal garden downstairs, it's like a pirate ship has just run aground, with sails flapping.

"Hello, Mrs Kosma," I say politely.

I wonder why she is here. She sometimes comes and has a general moan to Mum about the state of the bin area or the bloke directly above her who likes to play Queen's "We Will Rock You" ten times in a row when he gets back in from the pub.

But Mum isn't due in from work for at least another twenty minutes, and Mrs Kosma would know that, since she is the resident net-twitching, nosey old lady in our block of flats.

("Me? Oh, I just like to be friendly!" she'll explain, in her Big Fat Phoney old lady way.)

"Edith, your mama, she has asked me to come up here and look after you and Stanley," she says, taking a step forward, plainly expecting to come into our flat.

I don't move.

Why would Mum do that? As far as she knows, we've been picked up from school by some agency nanny. And I hadn't planned on letting her know that no one turned up till she got the chance to see that me and Stan have managed to look after ourselves without any help, thank you very much.

"Your mama, she called me when—"

BANG!

Mrs Kosma's explanation hangs in mid-air as we hear the main door to the flats slam closed and panicked high-heeled footsteps click-clack up the stairs to the first floor.

"Is that you, Justine?" Mrs Kosma calls out. "I am here with the children!"

Oh, how I *hate* being called a 'child'.

I am *so* not, and here's the proof:

- Every book I read comes from the Young Adult section of the library.
- I was chosen to be a buddy for a group of Year Sevens when they first started school and were lost and clueless.

- I've tried to make things better for Stan when no one else seemed to remember to.

When will anyone notice that I'm completely responsible?

"Yes, Mrs Kosma! And thank you!" Mum pants, her head appearing in view.

"Mum, it's OK!" I say, sensing the waves of panic emanating from her efficient navy suit as she hurtles towards us, her phone clutched in her hand and her knuckles as white as her nails are plum.

"Edie! Stan! What's going on?!" Mum yelps, breathlessly dropping down on to her knees to hug Stan and his knobbly armadillo.

"It's all right, Mum!" I tell her, trying to get a handle on the situation. "Me and Stan are just chilling out. And I've got tea on so everything's—"

"Do you know how *worried* I've been?!" Mum babbles, thunking her big bag down on the doormat (she should be careful with that – her laptop is in there). "Why didn't you answer your phone, Edie? Or the landline? I've been calling and calling!"

Oh. My mobile needed charging, so I pulled the plug out on the landline ... then forgot to stick the adaptor on (think I heard something good on the radio and went to turn it up).

"Well, it's just—" I try to begin, but Mum is too cross and stressed to listen to explanations.

"Do you *know* how I felt when the agency phoned me to apologize for their staff member being taken ill? I felt sick at the idea of Stan sitting alone with the teacher, the last to be collected. Then JUST as I'm about to call school, Miss Stewart phones to tell me that Stan sneaked out of the playground during a medical emergency with another child!"

"I was fine, Mum!" Stan says into her hair, since he is being cuddled very tightly indeed. "I'm a very big boy."

"Stan – a very big boy *doesn't* do something stupid like disappear! Do you know the police are on standby?"

"The police?" I gasp at Mum. "That's a bit dramatic, isn't it?"

"Dramatic?" says Mum, her blue eyes watery with tears of relief, but the muscles in her cheeks are also flexing with rage. "I'll tell you what's *dramatic*, Edie. When you think your youngest child has been abducted, and then you can't get hold of your

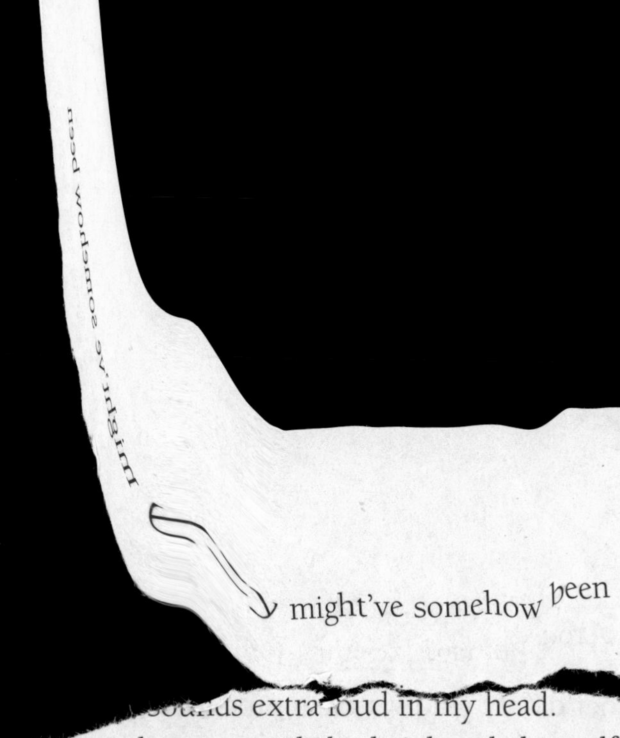

sounds extra loud in my head.

have to phone your dad – he's beside himself with worry," Mum suddenly mutters, pressing numbers into her phone behind Stan's back, so she's still semi-hugging him. "He's furious with me, of course. Blames me for not having someone dependable to look after you..."

"OK, I know I should have called you, Mum," I agree, "but me and Stan, we really don't need looking aft—"

PHEEEEEEEEEEEEEEEEEEEEEEEEEEEEEEEEEEEEEEEEEEEEEEEE!!!!!!!!!!!!!!!

We all wince and cover our ears as the fire alarm in the flat screeches in distress.

"Oh my!" shouts Mrs Kosma, waving a plump hand towards something behind me.

I turn and see smoke billowing from a doorway further along the hallway. I think the pasta might be a little overcooked...

"Oh, God!" yells Mum, as Mrs Kosma sets off for the kitchen at a cracking pace for someone so old and wide.

Frozen to the spot with fear or uselessness, I find

myself staring at Mum. With her
across her face like that, I can make
[illegible]
her dainty gold watch: ten past five.

Noticing that, I do a quick calculati[illegible]
estimate that it'll be roughly two or three hours ti[illegible]
she properly calms down and chills out, and about ten or twelve *years* till she trusts me to look after my brother by myself.

Where's a happiness clock when you need one?

'Cause I'd *love* to fast forward the hands to a time when everyone's forgotten about me setting fire to our flat.

A time when my mother can't remember that she once wanted to sack me as a daughter, like she does right now. . .

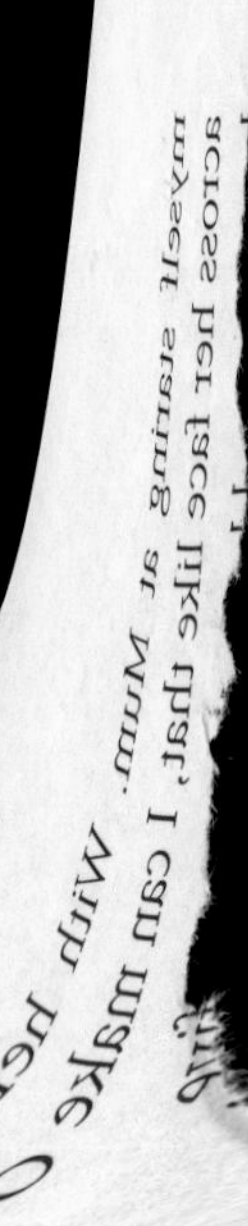

Chapter 4

Dear Old (Useless) Dad...

Q: What self-respecting thirteen-year-old goes to bed at eight o'clock on a Friday night?

A: One who is bored, bored, bored by the company of a gum-chewing so-called nanny.

So while Cheryl frantically chomps and texts in the living room, I'm in the top bunk in our hamster-sized bedroom at Dad's, reading by the light of my torch app.

Tippetty-tap! comes a light rapping at the door, and Dad is suddenly silhouetted in a chunk of light spilling in from the hall.

"Hi, Edie. Everything OK?" he whispers.

I see Dad look at his wrist, and spot a glow from his watch – he's checking how ridiculously late home he is.

"Yep, we're fine," I don't bother whispering back.

There's no point – Stan isn't asleep. He finds it hard to drift off in Dad's flat, since the multicoloured curtains are thin and the street-light on the canal path strobes right into our second-floor window, giving the room a disco feel. This would be fantastic if we fancied sticking on some sounds, but as our bedroom here is only big enough to fit in a bunk bed and nothing else, there's fat chance of a dance to go with it.

Plus Stan is a bit spooked by the flat, and likes it if I come to bed at the same time as him. (And I'm spooked by our bunk beds, but that's a different story.)

He gets especially spooked if Dad isn't home from work, like he wasn't tonight, not till a minute ago. We both heard his cheery hello to Cheryl, and her cheery hello back, as if she'd had a splendid few hours with us, instead of texting who-knows-who for four hours solid.

If you want to know about Stan's bad case of spooks, it goes back to the first night we came to sleep over. He held up Arthur, his pet crocodile, to look out of the window and they both got freaked by the sight of a dead swan floating in the canal.

I did try to explain to Stan (and Arthur) that it

was actually a large white Argos carrier bag, and therefore not at all morbid, but Stan couldn't get the thought of dead birds out of his head after that. In fact, he's been a bit funny about birds ever since, living *or* dead. (Or plastic.)

He's been doing a lot of backing away when we're near pigeons, which is a bit of a problem since Mrs Kosma likes to feed them crumbs out of her ground-floor bedroom window, right by the entrance to our block of flats, when she's not busy noseying at the neighbourhood or washing her collection of black pirate-sail dresses.

"So, Stan my man . . . not tired yet, buddy?" Dad says, dipping down out of my line of vision to talk to my brother.

Dad's not even taken his jacket off yet, he's been in such a rush to come and see us.

"Sort of but not really," I hear Stan say.

I carry on reading with the help of my torch app, though the glare of the street lamp means I hardly need it.

"Do you want to get up for a little while, then? It *is* Friday night, so no school tomorrow," Dad offers.

"Can we play Mousetrap?" I hear Stan ask hopefully.

"Er . . . well, we *could* put a DVD on," I hear Dad

say hesitantly. I know what's coming next. "It's just that I've got a bit of a deadline on, and I'll have to do some stuff on the computer."

It's always the same. Since Dad and his friend Eric set up their own website business, they seem to be working about twenty-seven hours a day. Dad warned Mum and us that it would be like this for the first couple of months, till the business got established. That was about a year ago. (Dad might be good at designing but he's obviously rotten at maths.)

Mum's not any better, of course. Her eyes went all shiny and she and Dad popped open a champagne bottle when she got her promotion. "Think of all the extra money I'll get!" she'd said, hugging me and Stan so tight we nearly spilled out celebratory Cokes.

And I guess the extra money *has* come in handy, to pay all the big fat phoney nannies who look after us while she works late. *And* the divorce lawyers, I guess.

"No, it's all right. . ." says Stan, pretending he's not disappointed. "Maybe I *am* a bit sleepy."

"OK, buddy," Dad replies, *also* sounding a bit disappointed. "What about you, Edie-beady-bear? Fancy hanging out with your dear old dad?"

What – and watch my dear old (useless) dad

twiddling with font options for an accountant's tastefully dull website? No, thanks . . . I might as well just lie here reading.

"Maybe in a while, once Stan's asleep," I lie. "But I'm a bit whacked."

It's been a tiring day, all right. All the most boring teachers seem to be saved up for Friday. (Tash had to nudge me awake in double French. She said I was snoring. I think it was 'cause I still had smoke from the burnt pasta swirling around in my head, blocking my sinuses.)

What I *don't* add is that I hate getting up and down the stupid ladder of this stupid bunk bed. I know it's hardly like climbing up the outside of the Eiffel Tower using only a grapple hook, but that's me. My head goes swirly with *any* kind of heights. Which is why once I'm up here, I lie straight down and don't get up again till morning.

(I *have* tried asking Stan to switch with me, but he's worried about being too far from his under-the-bed bundle of toys, and you can't argue with that sort of six-year-old logic, can you?)

"You two had a nice time with Cheryl?" Dad asks, determined to make small talk.

He's nodding his head in the direction of the

hallway, where I can hear Cheryl clattering about, gathering up her stuff to go home.

"Mm-hmm," I mumble non-committally.

We had as nice a time as we could, the three of us. I put nit shampoo on my hair and Stan's. Cheryl texted. I did my homework and helped Stan with his. Cheryl texted. I hit her with one of my (un)true actual facts, telling her that people who texted on a regular basis were ten times more likely to develop Attention Deficit Disorder. Cheryl went, "Huh?" and carried on texting. It was a riot.

"Look, tomorrow will be good," Dad promises, as he tries to squeeze my hand (I don't let go of my book). "I just need to get this work nailed tonight, then tomorrow, it'll be fun, fun, fun all the way!"

"What're we going to do, Dad?" Stan asks eagerly, dying to know what treats are in store.

"Uh..." Dad looks edgy, realizing he was supposed to have a plan for Stan, his little man, and his "Edie-beady-bear". (*Pur*-lease...)

"*Ayyyyyyyyyy-YIIIIIIIIIIIIIIII!*" comes a piercing scream, almost as loud as last night's fire alarm.

"Cheryl?!" shouts Dad in alarm, rushing out to see what's up.

"*Yessss!*" says a pleased small voice from the bunk

directly below me.

I flop my book down and whisper, "What did you do?"

I'm grinning. Stan is used to watching me subtly winding up and torturing nannies, and he's learned well. He is no longer just my accomplice. He is branching out on his own.

You want an example? Well, a couple of nannies ago, there was Susan, who had called his Lego "a terrible mess" a few too many times. After that, Stan had remembered her squirming at the sight of some bugs on a CBeebies nature programme. Next thing he's arranging a fine selection of plastic spiders on the toilet seat and closing the lid. I think I may have lost some of the hearing in my left ear due to the sheer volume of the screaming that came when Susan "nipped" to the loo. (She "nipped" out of our lives pretty soon after. . .)

"I said I didn't want any custard on my apple pie," Stan says, though he hasn't explained what he's actually done.

Outside, I can hear Cheryl loudly hyperventilating, while Dad is demanding to know what's wrong.

"You don't *like* custard," I reply, staring at the dangling bulb hanging from the ceiling, which Dad hasn't got round to buying a shade for yet.

"But then she *keeps* giving me custard, even though I say no really nicely," Stan carries on. "It's 'cause she's always texting and never listening."

In the hall, Cheryl is hiccupping, sobbing and trying to talk all at once. "Swarm! Swarm!" she seems to be saying. Are there lots of bees out there?! What *has* Stan been up to?

"Stan, what *exactly's* going on out there?" I ask my little brother.

"Well," says Stan, suddenly appearing – just eyes and freckly nose – by the edge of my bed. He must be balancing on the metal frame of his bunk. "You know how I came with you when you took the rubbish bag downstairs after tea?"

"Yes."

It just shows how insanely bored we got with Cheryl; taking the rubbish out seemed like a *treat*.

"Well, when you went into the bin area, I saw a little worm on the grass outside, and I thought it looked a little bit bored..."

Ah, now it's becoming clear.

"S'worm! It's a worm!" Cheryl is crying out. "Why is there a worm in my bag?"

"You put a *worm* in her handbag?" I say in

surprise and awe.

"Uh-huh!"

"But why didn't you tell me you were going to do that?"

"Thought it would be a nice surprise!" grins Stan – then he quickly thunks down to the floor as the bedroom door is flung open.

"Do either of you know anything—" Dad begins, looking stressed and cross.

"*Whaaaaaaaaahhhhhh!*" Stan instantly wails. "Why is someone screaming? I was sleeping! I'm scared!!"

Wow, what an actor. If Stan deserves merits for putting out the rubbish and stashing the worm, he should get at *least* another two for his award-winning performance there.

"Hey, easy tiger! It's OK – no need to panic," Dad says hurriedly, completely thrown off the scent and hugging his "traumatized" little boy.

"What *is* going on with Cheryl?" I ask Dad, as I prop myself up on my elbows (as much as I can manage without my head going spinny). "She's been acting really weird and jumpy since she picked us up."

"I don't know exactly," says Dad, holding Stan to his chest and gazing up at me in confusion. "She just said—"

BANG goes the front door.

"Cheryl?" Dad calls out, trying to extricate Stan from his arms, but Stan is having none of it.

He clings tightly to Dad and keeps on with the supremely convincing snivelling.

"CHERYL – HOLD ON!"

By the time Dad loosens Stan's iron grip and chases after her, the lift doors have clanged shut, and Cheryl is nowhere to be seen – unlike the worm, which is now wriggling on the hall table, alongside a hairbrush and a packet of half-finished chewing gum which got shaken out of Cheryl's bag in a hand-trembling panic.

Me and Stan hover in the bedroom doorway, grinning at each other.

"Fingers crossed?" says Stan, hopefully.

"Fingers crossed!" I answer more definitely, knowing *exactly* what he means.

Some wishes can't come true (like owning a genuine happiness clock).

But some miraculously can.

Oh yes; if me and Stan just believe in it, maybe this particular wish *will* come true.

Maybe this is the very, *very* last time we'll set eyes on Cheryl. . .

Chapter 5

Three Minutes Past Three

Fantasy, real life, historical, futuristic, horror, angels, funny, heartbreaking.

I'll read any kind of book.

(Except maybe ones about magic-eyed goats and vampire novels by a certain phoney writer.)

Out of all of those, I guess my *least* favourite is real life, if I had to choose. Maybe it's because the life I've got is a bit too "real" for my liking. . .

"Don't make a big deal out of it, Justine! It's only a *bit* early," Dad is hissing as he nods up at the huge library clock that hangs above the information desk. "You normally pick them up at five and it's only three o'clock now. It's just that I *have* to get this website design finished by the end of the day."

I pull out a book in the A-F section of the Young Adult bookshelves and peer at Mum and Dad through the gap. Behind them, people are serenely browsing the library shelves for books and DVDs. My well-practised parents are arguing in such a subtle way that no one – except me – has a clue that they are a small oasis of bitterness in an ocean of calm.

"Two hours can make a real difference, Neil! I've been working as well, you know – I've got to get ready for this conference next weekend, in case you'd *forgotten*." Mum hisses back, as she pats her giant slouch bag that's sure to be stuffed with designs and pads and lists of costings and calculations.

"Well, I hope you've remembered that I can't have the kids! Which nanny have you got looking after them?" Dad demands at low volume, folding his arms across his T-shirt. His hair is sticking up at a stupid, scruffy angle 'cause he hasn't had a shower yet today. I think he worked most of the night, and I know he worked most of this morning too. Yep, our fun, fun, *fun* day together consisted of me and Stan watching lots of Saturday-morning telly, then being taken to lunch in McDonald's. That was all right, but the way Dad went on – saying stuff like, "This is *great*, isn't it?" – you'd think he'd whisked us off to Disneyland Paris for the weekend.

"Don't you ever listen to what I'm saying, Neil? Miranda *quit*," Mum whispers with venom. "*And* the agency let me down. I've been through everyone on their list. I don't know *what* I'm going to do next week after school, never mind next weekend. What about your Cheryl? Could *she* look after them?"

In response, Dad presses a button on the phone he's holding and shows Mum something on the screen. What she reads makes her cover her face with her hands. (Yes, she *does* do that a lot.)

I know what Mum's just read. Cheryl texted Dad this morning to say she was doing a Miranda and quitting for good.

For Dad's sake – and to hide our guilt – me and Stan pretended to be shocked and surprised.

Though we *did* do a quick and careful high five as soon as he turned away to send her a please-don't-do-this text back.

(She replied with an absolutely-no-way-am-I-coming-back message in return.)

I suddenly hear a rumble of giggles coming from the children's section of the library – the Saturday afternoon story-time session must be going well.

Replacing the book in my spying spot, I back

away and go over to see what's got the little guys going, Stan included.

We arrived once the session had started and every centimetre of carpet space had a bottom on it, which is why he's at the back, leaning against a display full of picture books.

From where I'm standing, I can see that he's as lost in the silly story being told as any of the much younger kids, and I'm really pleased. He does NOT need to see or hear yet another sparring match between our parents, thank you very much. What he needs to hear – and snigger over – is a tale of aliens and their underpants, and anything else that gets a smile on his usually serious, freckly face.

With Stan happily occupied, I carry my chosen pile of books over to the checking-out desk. Someone up ahead is trying to reserve a book they want. The process seems to be taking a while, so quite a queue has built up.

I'm not in any hurry (certainly not in a hurry to go back and join Mum and Dad) so I find myself noseying at the noticeboard on the wall beside me.

On there are cards pinned up offering things for sale, like buggies, Sylvanian Families sets, arguing parents (only joking, sort of).

Flyers advertise toddler sing-along sessions, photo portraits of your kid, yoga for pregnant women (surely trying to bend with a bump would be as easy as cycling with your legs tied together?).

Info about various childminders, nannies and babysitters is stuck on there too. I recognize three:

1) Monique. She didn't think much of me and Stan simultaneously spilling our glasses of blackcurrant juice over her pile of wedding magazines. But then we didn't think much of her using our phone and computer to research trashy wedding bands and twee wedding favours when she was meant to be looking after us. And spilling those drinks at the same time *was* an accident. Honest.
2) Pauline. She insisted on regular inspections of our rooms for tidiness, homework for neatness and hair for nits. When I caught her arranging the tins in the kitchen cupboard in alphabetical order (beginning with "B" for beans and ending with "T" for tomatoes) I figured she was *way* too control-freaky for my liking. After that, me and Stan's rooms became much messier, along with our handwriting. The tins on the shelves

regularly got muddled up, and even seemed to flip themselves upside down. Stan showed Frances a hairbrush that was COVERED in nits, which turned *out* to be innocent grains of cous cous, we realized, after Frances had left (for ever). We have no idea how they got there. Honest.

3) Vicki. She lasted a week with us, till she left one day, crossing herself and muttering about "devil children". I have no idea why. I'm sure it had nothing to do with finding the Plasticine model I'd helped Stan make. I mean, *yes*, it looked a little like her (though if I say so myself, it was fantastically detailed, complete with a ponytail and glasses). And *yes*, we had stuck cocktail sticks into it. But it wasn't a REAL voodoo doll. Honest.

By the way, you know how Mum has that unusual version of a dictionary, where "amiable" means "horrible"? Well, I've got one of those too. And if you turn to the definition of "honest" in mine, it reads, "Yeah, *right*!"...

And today, amongst the Moniques, Paulines and Vickis, I notice a *new* ad.

You couldn't NOT notice it.

The rest are neatly printed on small rectangles of tidy white paper, but *this* one is handwritten – with each squiggly word a different colour – on a tatty yellow, heart-shaped Post-it.

With (how girly-girly is this) *diamante stickers* splodged around the edge. . .

I lean across to read the minuscule writing on this nuts-looking ad.

AM I WHO YOU'RE LOOKING FOR?
Need after-school childcare? You need ME!!
Please, please call Alice B. Lovely on. . .

I mean to stop reading when it comes to the phone number. I've seen enough to know this person is either mad or desperate or both.

But when I glance away and see that the book-reserving saga is continuing, I let my eyes drift back to the sparkles of diamante and reread the Post-it.

The hand-squiggled "y"s; the tails end in curlicues, I notice, like something a little kid would do.

And the name: *no one* has a dumb name like "Alice B. Lovely", unless they're maybe the daughter of an A-list celebrity.

Come to think of it, this might be the phoniest thing I've come across all week. It's as if someone is trying to sound cutesy and appealing to every gushy, overprotective mum going. It's a wonder this "Alice B. Lovely" person doesn't have a photo of herself hugging adorable babies while blowing bubbles. . .

Blat!

Mum's hand lands star-shaped beside the Post-it heart.

"*Don't*," I say firmly, certain I know what's coming next, "even *think* about this one. . ."

I do not need some BFP nanny who had the mental age of a kitten telling me (and Stan) what to do.

"But Edie, darling, look at the note. She might be quite a *fun* sort of person!"

"Look at the note *again*," I answer her. "She might be a *psychopath*."

And Mum might be desperate. She'd never have been tempted by something so home-made, unprofessional and ridiculous before. But then I guess me and Stan have been through just about every nanny within a ten-mile radius of here (and broken them all).

"Well, I wouldn't say it was *psychopathic*," Mum

says, though she's squinting a bit more dubiously at the Post-it, I'm pleased to see.

"The person who did that is loopy, and not safe to be left with children," I announce. "It's a known fact that adults who write in this childlike way have serious mental health issues. We did it in psychology. Honest!"

Mum's mouth twitches with uncertainty, her desperation clashing with my unwanted truths/lies.

"OK, OK," Mum mutters, giving up on Alice B. Lovely.

Or so I think.

The time is three minutes past three, and three things are happening simultaneously. . .

1) The queue to the check-out desk moves forward at last.
2) Mum secretively taps something into her phone.
3) I get a sick feeling in the pit of my stomach.

(*Please* don't let her be doing what I *think* she's doing. . .)

Chapter 6

"Am I Who You're Looking For?" (No)

It's been a really nice afternoon.

No, really.

Not a shred of sarcasm meant, not this once.

I came out of after-school club with Tash, and there was Stan, waving his arms like a windmill gone bonkers. And beside him was no unknown nanny; it was Mum, smiling in her sensible navy suit, her bulging leather sack-bag hanging heavy on her shoulder.

"What are you doing here?" I asked in surprise, while Tash showed Stan the latest photos of Max on her phone. (Max chewing a bone, Max chasing pigeons, Max chewing a pigeon. Only joking. . .)

Before she'd dropped us at our breakfast clubs this morning, Mum had been scanning some local mums' website or other for emergency nannies.

Obviously she hadn't had any luck. As Stan would say, "Yessssss!"

(And *I* was thinking "Yessssss!" 'cause that *also* meant Mum hadn't taken the cutesy yellow Post-it note and its owner seriously yesterday.)

"My boss was fine about me coming home early today," she explained.

"Really?" I said incredulously.

Mum's boss at Indigo Dove (nice name, horrible "casual" clothes for middle-aged women) is in her twenties, with no children, and thinks everyone should work every waking hour, and possibly a little bit more, or they're slacking.

The idea that she was "fine" about Mum sloping off to meet us from school sounded about as likely as my parents having a laugh and a joke together.

"Yes, really!" Mum nodded. "I just thought, hey, let's not stress about getting some last-minute childcare sorted today. I'll bunk off early and hang out with my gorgeous kids!"

I eyed Mum suspiciously for telltale signs of lying. Nothing. Either she was fantastically good at fibs (like me) or she was telling the truth.

"Fancy coming back for tea with us?" she asked

Tash. "Fish and chips? With a stop-off for an ice lolly on the way?"

Tash said yes, all giddily giggly.

And then *I* got a bit giddy, to be honest (I mean *really* honest, not weird dictionary honest). It's just that Mum hadn't sounded so upbeat and, well, old-skool Mum for months. I think I'd become so used to the tight-lipped, tense version of her that I'd forgotten this one existed.

And so we bought ice lollies, and Mum didn't even mind when a bit of her Magnum glooped on her expensive suit.

The four of us talked and giggled all the way home, taking turns to throw the hand-burningly hot bundle of fish and chips to each other, like an edible, vinegary rugby ball.

Back at the flat, we sat round the table, passing the ketchup, stealing each other's chips, chatting about Max and school and Stan's upcoming homework project (he wants to do it on crocodiles, or Lego, of *course*).

So, like I say, it's been really nice.

Till now.

'Cause the doorbell has just rung, and Mum's face has gone funny.

It's like in a film, where there's an ominous knock at the door, and the heroine – as well as the viewers – all know the bad guy is standing outside, and he *hasn't* come to deliver a pizza.

"What's wrong?" I frown at Mum, as she hurriedly squeaks back the chair and gets up.

"Nothing!" she says extra-brightly, like heroines in movies do, when they're trying to pretend to their kids that everything is OK, and there's not really an assassin standing on the front doormat. (*Please* don't let there be an assassin standing on our front doormat!)

As Mum hurries off, I realize Tash and Stan are staring at me.

"Why did you ask what was wrong?" says Tash.

Stan doesn't have to say anything. The familiar look of sheer worry is in his Malteser-brown eyes. I sometimes (but don't often) forget he looks to me to assure him that our world is all right.

"It's nothing. I got muddled. I meant to say, 'Who could that be?' but it came out, er, wrong," I lie quickly, hoping that'll do for a cover-up.

Luckily, it does.

The tension goes out of Stan's face and he carries

on walking a chip up a set of Lego stairs that he's made and jumps it into his mouth.

Tash knows better and stays silent, listening, like I am, for whoever's at the door.

"Ah, hello!" we hear Mum's voice say.

I can't properly hear what's being said back, or by who – Mum's got her iPod on some happy, pop-ish shuffle. I get up and hurry over to the dock, swirling the sound down on Beyoncé.

As soon as there's silence (well, nearly silence, if you don't count Stan's "One . . . two . . . three . . . WHEEEE!" sound effects, as the chips climb 'n' jump) I hear footsteps in the hall. Two sets.

Pleased to meet you, Mr Assassin! (Yes, I've been reading too many spies-in-jeopardy novels recently.)

". . .and do you live nearby?" Mum is asking.

It doesn't *seem* like the sort of question you put to a cold-blooded killer.

"Just the other side of the park," I hear the whoever answer, in a soft, girly voice.

It could be a cunning disguise, of course, but it doesn't *sound* much like the sort of voice a cold-blooded killer might have. But you can never be sure.

"Edie? Stan? I've got someone I want you to meet," says Mum, breezing into the kitchen.

Uh-oh. . .

It's as if the world stops whirling for a moment.

I picture the sharp, pointy hands of the clock of doom in the hall juddering to a sudden halt.

Everything feels like it's turned 4D.

Mum and Tash and the kitchen are all still here, but fuzzy, fading into the background.

In this strange fourth dimension, there's just me, and a small boy with a sauce-dripping chip stopped in mid-air, mid-jump.

And in front of us, in high definition, is the craziest-looking girl I've ever seen.

She can't be much older than me. Sixteen, maybe? Seventeen at the oldest? But I've never seen anyone like her before.

Her long fair hair is all one length, parted in the middle, hanging like shiny curtains, with just a hint of an ear peeking through on one side.

She's wearing some retro belted tweedy beige jacket with a big furry cream collar that puffs up behind her neck like a fuzzy version of an Elizabethan ruff.

Her skirt is something scarlet and silky and antique-looking, with a hint of frilly petticoat showing underneath.

There are fuchsia pink tights and beat-up gold Mary Jane shoes; the sort of shoes you'd see on 1920s flapper girls in vintage black and white movies on the History Channel.

But it's not the fact that she looks like she ran into the wardrobe room of a theatre company blindfolded and came out wearing the first things she found.

It's her face. . . She looks like a doll.

Not some knowing, mascara'd Bratz doll, I mean. More like the slightly spooky porcelain one that used to be in the glass china cabinet at Nana's old house; the kind of precious, delicate doll that grannies and great-grannies had as children and were never allowed to play with because they'd break. (Same goes for grandchildren.)

Milk-pale, round-faced dolls with rosebud mouths, dainty penny-sized flushes of pink on their cheeks and wide, weird glassy gazes staring at you.

One of those wide, weird glassy gazes is staring at me now. The most unbelievable eyelashes surround eyes that are the most unusual sea green. The lashes are long, black and *sparkling*, radiating the tiniest sprinkles of light, as if this girl has minuscule shards of mirrorball glued to the tips.

Chime!

The clock of doom springs back into life, letting us know that it's quarter past six.

"And *this*," I hear Mum's voice say, as the dimensions shift back into something approaching normal, "is Alice B. Lovely."

BOING!!

That's the sound of a frying pan of obviousness hitting the side of my head.

Mum didn't just decide to quit work early on a whim.

She had it all planned.

She was contacting this Alice B. Lovely person on her email this morning, *not* searching internet mums' sites for last-minute nannies.

She's come home early so we could all be here, so we could all meet Alice B. Lovely together.

How *lovely*.

Honestly.

(You can guess which version of honestly I mean here. . .)

My turn for kisses.

"Night, night, then!" I say to Stan, as I tuck him and Arthur in and remove the knobbly Lego armadillo that he's tried to take to bed.

"Night, night, Edie!" says Stan, as I plonk a smacker on his forehead.

"Light on, or off?" asks Mum, with a hand on the Arsenal table lamp on top of his chest of drawers.

My brother used to demand pitch-blackness before he could get to sleep. But he's been more nervy lately, more prone to bad dreams (head-twisting stuff like finding teeth in an apple and white bird feathers in his pockets).

"On," he insists.

"See you in the morning, love," says Mum, as she drifts out.

"Yeah, see you, Stan," I say, about to turn and go.

"Edie! Edie!" Stan whispers urgently, grabbing hold of the bottom of my shirt.

"Uh-huh?" I murmur. I don't mind staying and chatting for a bit with Stan. It puts off going to the living room and having to chat to Mum (no guesses what she'll want to talk about).

"That girl today . . ." he begins.

So he wants to talk about her too. I was hoping we could pretend that Alice B. Lovely and her crazy, phoney false eyelashes was just a figment of our imaginations.

". . . what . . . what *was* she?"

"A freak," I reply, matter-of-factly.

"Oh," says Stan, sounding a little disappointed.

"What's the 'Oh' for, buddy?" I ask my brother more gently, using one of Dad's many nicknames for him.

"I just thought ... maybe ... she was sort of *special.*"

"Special?" I snap, my gentleness instantly evaporating. "Why exactly?"

In the twenty minutes Alice B. Lovely had sat and had a juice and cake with us, I'd found out several things:

1) She is sixteen, i.e. three years older than me.
2) She has never done any after-school "childcare" before – just babysat a bunch of neighbours' kids when they were fast asleep (which isn't so much babysitting as watching telly in someone else's house, as far as I'm concerned).
3) She said "please" and "thank you" so much to my mother that I felt like vomiting. She's either so nice it's untrue, or it really is untrue and she's a BFP out to spoof my mum into giving her a job.

There is no *way* I want an inexperienced BFP who is practically *my* age looking after me. Specially one dressed like an explosion in a fancy dress shop.

"I liked her eyes and her eyelashes," Stan carries on dreamily. "And her hair was all silky. And so was her skirt. And did you see her shoes? They were gold! Have you ever seen gold shoes, Edie?"

"No, but—"

"And best of all, I liked the way she made me a diving board!"

Mum had done all the talking really, explaining the hours and the wages and the fact that if she accepted the job, Alice B. Lovely would have to take us to Dad's as well this week, till he sorted himself out with more childcare help in the absence of Cheryl.

She twittered on about the times of our respective after-school clubs, the addresses of our schools and what we liked for tea.

She yakked about how good Alice B. Lovely's references were from her neighbours.

Through all mum's endless talking and twittering and yakking, Alice B. Lovely sat still and wide-eyed, only interjecting with a "Yes, Mrs Henderson", "No,

Mrs Henderson", "Please, Mrs Henderson" and "Thank you, Mrs Henderson" here and there.

Then at one point – still hanging on Mum's every word – she reached over to Stan's Lego tub, which was sitting on the table next to him, rifled around in it, and pulled out a long flat red piece. As she nodded and smiled at what Mum was saying, she clipped the piece on to the chin-high set of Lego steps he'd made, automatically transforming the whole thing into a diving board. She then grabbed a chip, walked it up the steps and made it do a double somersault *straight* into Stan's gaping mouth.

Of *course* my little brother was going to think that was special. He was only six. He couldn't see that down the line, she'd be as uninterested in us and as phoney with our parents as all the others.

"Now come on, Stan. We *have* to stick to our plan," I remind him. "We don't *need* anyone looking after us!"

I try to forget the blackened pan that's now in the communal bins downstairs (no amount of soaking got the burnt bits of pasta off).

I also try to forget the moment at the kitchen table when my mum said, "Well, I don't know what *you* think, Alice, but – in answer to your Post-it note question – yes, I think you ARE the one we're looking for!"

Mum had beamed around at us as if she'd made a tremendously funny joke, rather than a tremendously big mistake.

Only Tash smiled back, mainly because it wasn't going to be HER getting picked up by a freak in fancy dress every day from school. . .

"That would be lovely!" said Alice B. Lovely, blinking her sparkling eyelashes so hard that it seemed as if her eyes were actually glittering.

"OK, Edie," Stan says solemnly now, cuddling Arthur by the neck.

"Just me and you against the world, remember?" I tell him, holding my pinky finger out for him to shake with his.

"Me and you against the world!" he repeats, linking pinkies with me.

I give him (and Arthur) another quick kiss and then head towards the living room.

Mum is kneeling down in front of the DVD player, studying it as if it's a bear trap. She's never been able to understand how it works beyond sticking the DVD in.

"Why are there so many buttons on these things?"

she grumps, about to press something she shouldn't that'll change the neon green timer if she's not careful.

"Here, let me," I say, snatching the remote from the table and activating the DVD player with a whirr and soft clink.

Dad always had to do the techno stuff like this. He'd grumble, but I think he quite liked it, since he always moaned about Mum being a know-all when it came to everything else in our lives.

For years, he used to say that in a gentle, teasing sort of way. But towards the end, he'd say it in a bitter and biting sort of way.

"Thanks," says Mum with a warm smile. "And Edie, I think this is going to turn out all right, you know."

"Well, of course it is. We've watched it already!" I say, nodding at the corny rom com she's clutching. "I could probably recite *every* line in the last scene."

"No, not the *film*!" Mum laughs. "I'm talking about Alice B. Lovely. Don't you think she's just . . . I don't know . . . *delicious*? I have this really funny feeling about her!"

"Wow, what a coincidence." I tell Mum through gritted teeth. "'Cause *I* have a really funny feeling about her as well."

A funny feeling that she's going to be the most useless, weird and phoney nanny of the lot.

"Do you, darling? Well, that's great!" Mum beams.

She's obviously got her sarcasm radar switched off for the night.

I think about bursting her bubble and pointing out how irresponsible she is to leave us with yet another stranger, especially one who's clearly a weirdo, but I've run out of energy.

Instead I flop down on the sofa and get ready to squirm at the movie, feeling as miserable and defeated as possible.

DONG! goes the clock of doom in the hallway, striking the first of several depressing clangs to let us know it's eight o'clock.

And with every dull *DONG!* my heart sinks, sinks, *sinks*.

I feel like it's reminding me that I'm still a *long* way off winning the nanny wars. . .

Chapter 7

Life According to Edith P Henderson

The time is one minute to humiliation.

After-school club today has mostly consisted of Year Sevens for some reason, and I don't care too much what they might think of me, *or* the freakoid nanny who's waiting over by the gate with my little brother.

But irritatingly, I *do* care what Cara Connelly, Dionne Omiata and Holly King think.

Here are three facts you need to know about these girls:

1) They are in sixth form (no school uniform; they're all micro-minis, ballet pumps and a ton of make-up).
2) They are gorgeous, in a glam way (see above).
3) They are Big Fat Phonies (you should see how they suck up to the teachers, while treating

anyone below them in school like they're as important as dust molecules).

The trouble is, Cara, Dionne and Holly's opinion seems to matter to virtually everyone I know, including me. (Sad but true.)

When I first started at secondary and was sitting in the dinner hall, getting to know my new classmates, they passed by just as someone asked what the "P" of my middle name stood for.

"Pathetic?" one of them had giggled to another.

I was gutted. (*Also* sad but true.)

My middle name is actually Patricia, after my nana. But it might as well be P for pathetic, 'cause quite often I am, as you'll see. . .

"Hey, check out Dionne's nails!" whispers Tash, nodding towards the gang of three as they amble elegantly out of the sixth-form block.

"Yuck," I mumble.

Dionne is holding up her hands and fanning her fingers out, so her girlfriends can see her new false nails, which are very long, very colourful and very *clawed*. Why do people think that's such a good look? When Linzee (nanny number four or five) used to tap *hers* in annoyance, all I could think of was how complicated it must be to do normal stuff like go to the loo. ("*Or* pick your nose," Stan once said very sagely.)

But I'm less horrified by Dionne's creepy nails and more horrified because we seem to be on a collision course: me and Tash, Dionne and her mates . . . our paths set to merge *right* at the gate.

And the only people waiting to pick up today are one Turkish granny, who's wearing a black sail dress very similar to Mrs Kosma's, a bored dad in a grey suit, a small boy in a blue blazer who looks a lot like Stan (because he *is* Stan) and a girl so bizarrely dressed she stands out like a parakeet in a flock of starlings.

Alice B. Lovely is wearing the same furry-collared beige jacket, but her skirt this time is electric blue, with some kind of print on it that I can't quite make out from here. Her tights are jade green, and the shoes are dark red velvet wedges. Each thing is pretty nice, maybe something you'd see in the vintage section of the huge Topshop flagship store in London. (Never been; just read about it in a magazine.)

The thing is, the Topshop assistants who dress the dummies . . . they'd never put all that particular stuff *together*.

And please don't let Dionne and the others put me, Stan and Alice B. Lovely together, I stress silently.

They've spotted her already, of course. Who wouldn't? The Turkish granny is looking her up and down as if she's found herself standing next to a martian. The grey-suited dad is a lot less bored and more confused now that he's glanced up from his phone and seen this doll-faced apparition.

"Check out the eyelashes!" we hear Cara say, nudging Dionne, who mutters what must be the same remark to Holly.

Oh, yes, we are close enough to see that today's eyelashes are different from yesterday's.

"Purple!" squeaks Tash, spotting them too.

(By the way, if you want a time check, it's now two seconds to humiliation.)

"Edie!" yelps Stan, doing his bonkers windmill act.

Relax, I tell myself. *That's all right. That's just a little kid shouting out. Super-cool sixth-form girls aren't going to pay attention to that.*

But now Alice B. Lovely is lifting her hand – a hand in a silver glove, for goodness' sake – and wiggling her fingers my way.

OK, *that's* done it.

Three heads, with flickably long hair, swivel round to see who the freaky girl at the gate is waving at.

And since there is only me and Tash here, and Tash isn't the one with the bright red face, I think they have a pretty good idea that the freak belongs to *me*. . .

There's only one thing to do: brazen it out.

"Hey, Edie!" chirps Stan, as I reach the gate.

"Uh-huh," I mutter blankly, walking as fast as I can with my head held as high as it's physically possible before it starts tilting backwards.

"Hello," I hear Alice B. Lovely's little-girl-voice say.

But her hello is somewhere behind me. I've already swooped past her and Stan and am stomping off down the road towards home.

"Edie?" Stan's confused voice calls after me, but I am not going to look back, specially not so I can see the sniffy expressions on Cara, Dionne and Holly's faces.

Stan and old whatshername will just have to catch up with me, like Tash has just done.

"What are you up to?" she says breathlessly, falling into step beside me.

I'm a bit disappointed with her question, actually. I thought she knew me well enough to feel my humiliation and spot my escape tactics. And hadn't we spent most of our free time today talking about the weirdness of my new so-called nanny?

"Duh! I'm going home!" I answer her, my eyes staring straight ahead.

In the distance is the parade of shops where Mum bought us ice lollies yesterday. What a great, spontaneous surprise that had seemed. (Or rotten, phoney plot to butter me up, more like.)

"But Edie!" Tash says urgently. "Edie, it's Tuesday! You're going to your dad's tonight, remember?"

Ugh.

My footsteps slow down.

I have no choice. No choice but to turn and walk the walk of shame *back* towards the parakeet girl and my little brother, who are standing waiting for me, one looking confused, the other . . . just doll-like and patient.

Dionne's elbow thunks mine as the three sixth formers sashay past me arm-in-arm-in-arm, sniggering.

"See you tomorrow!" Tash calls after me.

Yes, of course.

Unless I curl up and die through sheer embarrassment before then. . .

"Tell me something else."

"M&M's! Blue ones!"

The Tell-Me-Something-Else game has been going on all the way to Dad's. Stan says something he likes, and Alice B. Lovely asks him to Tell Her Something Else. So far he's mentioned Lego, Christmas, peas, Arthur, crocodiles, Horrid Henry, pass-the-parcel, pine cones, ABBA songs, Luke Skywalker, trampolines, stars, mint-choc-chip ice cream and socks with cartoon characters on them, amongst a zillion other things.

"Hey, how about *you* tell me something else, Edie?" says Alice B. Lovely.

"How can I tell you something else?" I answer, without taking my eyes off the book I've been reading while walking. (Not easy. I nearly tripped up a bunch of times.)

"You just say a thing you like, Edie!" Stan encourages me, not realizing that I'm trying to make a point.

"But I can't say something *else*, Stan, can I?" I tell him firmly. "Not if I haven't said anything in the *first* place, since I'm not *playing*."

I know that sounds petty and stubborn. At least I *hope* it sounds petty and stubborn to Alice B. Lovely, so she gets off my case with the let's-be-friends silly games.

"OK," says Alice B. Lovely, in an infuriatingly untroubled way. "Back to you, Stan! Tell me something else! A colour, this time."

"Um . . . purple! Like your eyelashes!" Stan blurts out.

Out of the corner of my eye, I see Alice B. Lovely smile and bat her fluffy purple eyelashes.

Suddenly I feel a bit cross with Stan. What's he playing at? Is he genuinely sucking up to her? Or is he lulling her into a false sense of security, and when she least expects it, he'll hit her with a hidden worm or scattering of spiders, maybe?

I'd like to think it's the second option, but it's looking worryingly like the first, from where I'm standing.

And I happen to be standing at the entrance to Dad's small block of flats.

"We're here," I say flatly, lifting my finger to the entry-code keypad.

The main door is on the street side, not the canal side, so I can't spot whatever random bits and disgusting bobs might be floating in the water.

"Tell me something else," Alice B. Lovely says to Stan, not acknowledging what *I've* just said. "A person, this time."

"Edie!" says Stan, without a moment's hesitation, which makes me adore him all over again, despite the sucking up.

"Tell me something else!" Alice B. Lovely prattles on, as the door swings open and we enter the foyer.

"Racing Edie up the *stairs*!" Stan calls out, and next thing he's flying by me, his school bag thwacking me into action.

"Oh no, you don't, Stanley Henderson!" I shout, hurtling after him.

We're both giggling and breathless when we reach the door on the second floor, but I already have the key in my hand and we fall into the hall together, deliberately trying to trip each other up as we bumble to the kitchen to dump our bags and grab some water from the tap.

"Me first! I'm the littlest!" says Stan, pulling the arc-shaped mixer tap round towards him.

"Sorry – *me* first, since I'm your elder and better!" I tell him, shoving his head away with my hand and quickly drinking from the gushing cold flow.

"Hey, you two are fast!"

In our bubble of silliness, I'd forgotten she was there for a second.

And now I feel properly stupid, with my cheek, chin and shirt collar wet from the water.

Wiping the drips from my face, I stare at Alice B. Lovely properly for the first time today.

In Dad's ultra modern, ultra sheeny-shiny white kitchen, with her mismatching second-hand everything, she looks even more odd than ever.

Like someone from a different time; a long-ago decade.

Maybe it's the vintage pattern on her swirly electric blue skirt: I can see now that it's made up of flamingos. Lots and lots of flamingos. A. . .

"A 'stand' of flamingos!" Alice B. Lovely announces. "That's how you're meant to describe them!"

Excuse me, but did she just read my mind? I fret, as she twists and swirls her skirt around her, and looks fondly at the ridiculously pink and gangly birds.

"I saw you looking," says Alice B. Lovely, flicking her eyes from her skirt and aiming her gaze straight at me.

Do I feel better that she's said that? Or am I a little worried that she's just read my mind *again*?

And those eyes – there's something . . . odd going

on with them. They're almost as violet as her lashes. But I thought her eyes were—

"Don't you just love collective nouns?" she says brightly.

Don't you just love collective nouns? Who says stuff like that?! A total BFP, *that's* who.

I pick my novel back up from where I dumped it by my school bag and plonk myself down on the nearest stool. It's the vampire book I got signed by the BFP author-who-I-won't-name. So far, it's not very good (or maybe I've just decided not to like it), but *anything* is better than listening to Alice B. Lovely wittering away.

"What's a klective nine?" I hear Stan ask, as I flip to the bookmark.

"Group names for things. They're sometimes pretty funny," says Alice B. Lovely, taking her jacket off to reveal a skinny-rib, ruby-coloured polo neck and a giant double cherry pendant dangling from a long silver chain.

She strolls over to join Stan at the kitchen sink in a few dainty steps of her red velvet wedges. "Here's one I like . . . a 'glint' of goldfish!"

Stan grins.

"A 'clutter' of spiders!" she says next.

Stan grins some more.

"A 'mess' of iguanas!"

Stan grins till his freckles practically disappear in the crinkles round his nose.

"A 'charm' of magpies!"

Stan giggles, which is pretty amazing since he doesn't even like birds.

"They sound made up," I mumble in as bored a voice as I can manage, without looking up from my book. (I quickly swivel it the right way round, and hope Alice B. Lovely doesn't notice.)

"Nope, they're all real. Real as you and me," says Alice B. Lovely, looking back over her shoulder at me and smiling.

Real? I'm not sure Alice B. Lovely can totally describe herself that way. Those eyelashes aren't exactly natural, for a start. Which brings me on to something else. . .

"Hey, why don't *you* tell us something?" I challenge Alice B. Lovely.

"OK," she says serenely.

"Why have your eyes changed colour? Weren't your eyes pale green yesterday?"

"Yes," she nods. "They're coloured contact lenses. Aren't they cool?"

She turns to Stan and opens her eyes wide. He stares practically nose-to-nose at her pupils and wows a bit, then suddenly says, "Tell us something else!"

"Hmm . . . well, my favourite colour is yellow, but that wouldn't look too good for an eye colour, I don't think."

Yellow. She *would* like that. All phoney bright. Yellow is a BFPC (Big Fat Phoney *Colour*).

"Tell us something else!" Stan grins.

"Let's see . . . how about art? Art is my favourite subject at school."

"I love art too!" says Stan excitedly. "But tell me something else!"

"Ooh. . ." murmurs Alice B. Lovely, glancing around the room for inspiration. Her eyes settle on the cooker. "I love Quattro Formaggio pizza – it's my favourite food."

Then, seeing Stan's look of confusion, she adds, "It means four types of cheese".

"Yew – Edie would *hate* that. She doesn't like cheese, do you?"

Stan and Alice B. Lovely wait for me to answer, but I pretend to be reading my book.

"Tell me something else!" he starts again.

"Er . . . magpies. I love them."

"Stan hates birds," I mutter darkly, but maybe a bit too quietly – neither of them seems to have heard me.

"*I* remember. A 'charm' of magpies!" Stan says, and giggles at his cleverness.

"That's right, Stan. And hey, *I* just remembered something," says Alice B. Lovely, slapping her hand on the draining board. "Crocodiles . . . it's a '*bask*' of crocodiles!"

Stan immediately rushes over to his school bag and pulls out Arthur, who's been shoved in there along with his pencil case and packed lunch.

"Hear that, Arthur?" he tells his squashy, much-loved friend. "Arthur, meet Alice B. Lovely. Arthur comes from Kenya, where there are *lots* of crocodiles! My uncle went on a safari there last year and brought him back for me. Arthur likes cuddles. . ."

Aw . . . Stan is too cute. (As long as he doesn't think it's all right to cuddle *real* crocodiles, otherwise we're in BIG trouble next time we go to a zoo.)

You know, I remember that visit from Uncle Bob; he brought *me* back a toy hippo. You can guess how many times I cuddled *that*. . . (Clue: it was between zero to one times.)

"Pleased to meet you, Arthur," says Alice B. Lovely, shaking one green paw. "You know, my dad's been on safari."

"Did he go to Kenya too?" asks Stan.

"No, not Kenya. Not that far. . ." she says dreamily, then lets her gaze shift to the window above the sink. "Your dad must love living here, with this view!"

I think my dad preferred the view he had at our old flat, his old home. Staring at a stagnant puddle of brown canal water can't make up for the fact that he's living in a tiny apartment on his own all week, except for the couple of nights me and Stan stay over.

"Yeah, it's great if you enjoy watching rubbish bobbing by," I say, irritated to see Alice B. Lovely now making herself at home. She's moved away from the sink and is unlocking the door that leads out on to the balcony.

I'm even more irritated to see Stan trot after her.

Reluctantly following them, I lean on the door frame and stare a hole in the back of Alice B. Lovely's head. Her silky straight hair is beautiful. Next time Stan gets nits, I'll have to get him to rub his head against hers. . .

"There were three shopping trollies in there last week, weren't there, Stan?" I say.

"Maybe a 'tangle' of shopping trollies, eh, Stan?" Alice B. Lovely laughs softly.

Stan laughs too. It wasn't even funny. I wish my brother would just stop with all the grinning and giggling and laughing.

"Or a 'rattle' of shopping trollies, 'cause that's the sound they make!" he takes a turn to suggest.

"Nice one!" she says, lifting her silver-gloved hand up for a high five, which Stan obligingly slaps. (What?!)

"Dog walkers sometimes throw doggy poo bags in there as well," I tell her.

I don't know why I'm only mentioning the yucky stuff. Me and Stan, we have a list of the funny things we've seen bobbing along. Like the hamster ball (luckily, minus a hamster inside), the boogie board (no one was going to be catching any waves in *this* particular stretch of water any time soon), and a giant inflatable palm tree (we fished it out with a broken branch from one of the nearby cherry trees, but ended up bursting it).

The trouble is, I often just get stuck in this habit of coming out with the most negative stuff possible. Or the sarkiest. Specially in the company of unwanted nannies.

"I bet you see beautiful things too," says Alice B. Lovely. "Ducks and swans. . ."

Uh-oh. Wrong thing to mention in front of Stan.

"We saw a dead swan in there once," he replies.

I should correct him, remind him it was just a plastic Argos carrier bag. But I'm quite keen for the perfect(ly strange) Alice B. Lovely to think she's said the wrong thing.

"It's given him nightmares," I tell her. "He gets creeped out by birds now."

"Oh, but Stan – birds are beautiful," Alice says, blinking her feathery eyes. "Can you imagine how it must feel to soar up in the sky?"

What on earth is she doing now? She's standing on the little ledge that runs around the balcony, pressing herself against the railings, and has her arms out wide.

Stan is staring at her as if she's gone stark raving bananas.

"Come on, Stan – we're at the same height as the birds here. See how it feels!"

She glances around, sees an empty window box and tips it upside down. Next thing, Stan is standing on it, tummy pressed against the railings, arms outstretched.

He giggles self-consciously.

"See that pigeon?" says Alice B. Lovely, and Stan nods. "Well, just copy the way it swoops!"

So Stan swoops, stiffly at first, but Alice B. Lovely stands behind him, puts her arms under his and starts to bob, weave and glide.

It's like watching some corny move a CBeebies presenter might do.

"Cooo!" says Alice B. Lovely.

Help – she's doing pigeon noises. Kill me *now*.

"*You* try it, Stan."

Don't, Stan! I urge him under my breath.

"Coooo!" says Stan. "Coooo!"

No. . .

I stand in stunned silence for a few seconds, watching from behind as my brother and this very strange stranger waft from side to side making ridiculous sounds.

A couple of very gullible pigeons flutter close by, lured by the cooing, though maybe they're just as confused as me and want a better look at the crazy humans.

"OI!!!!!"

The real pigeons flap off in a panic of wings and loose feathers.

The fake ones drop their arms and look at the source of the shouting.

I bound forward too, recognizing my dad's voice in a heartbeat.

"GET AWAY FROM THE EDGE, FOR GOD'S SAKE!" he's yelling from the bridge that crosses the canal a little further up. "DON'T YOU REALIZE HOW DANGEROUS THAT IS?"

Oh, yeah . . . I guess from *his* angle it might look more like Stan is about to dive head first into the canal.

From *his* angle, Dad wouldn't have seen that Stan was perfectly safe, wedged between the railings and Alice B. Lovely.

From *my* angle, it seems like Alice B. Lovely is on a countdown to a big shout-down with my dad.

Hurray!

Anything that makes things uncomfortable for nannies is fine by me.

That might sound harsh, but that's just life, according to Edith P. Henderson.

And Alice B. Lovely better get used to it, or get lost.

(I'd prefer the second option, please. . .)

Chapter 8

The Art of Litter

I have a headache.

It's lasted for, let's see, nearly three months now.

It starts the second my alarm clocks shrills on at seven-thirty a.m.

That's when I open my eyes and have a blast of Dulux Lemon Tropics sear my retinas.

"It's lovely!" said Tash, when she came and saw my formerly cream-coloured bedroom walls painted vivid yellow by my temporarily insane mother. "Like sunshine!"

She *would* say that, obviously. Tash tries to put a good spin on everything. Like when her old dog Sid died, she said, "At least he's not in pain any more. . ."

Then when my parents split up, she said, "Well, at least you won't have to listen to them arguing and throwing mugs at each other."

If an asteroid was about to hit the planet and wipe out mankind, she'd probably say, "Well, at least Mum won't expect me to tidy my room today. . ."

And when *my* mum went a bit loopy after Dad moved out and painted every room in the flat the sort of colours used in Year 1 art lessons, my loyal, ever upbeat best friend said, "Well, it'll be nice to wake up to such a – a *fizzy* colour in the mornings."

Fizzy? Well, I guess it was a bit like being woken with a mouth full of sherbet every day.

"Does this colour come with a free pair of extra-strength sunglasses?" I asked Mum, when me and Stan came back from a week at Nana's new house, not long after Dad had moved out. (It was a *long* week. I love my nana, but her bungalow isn't exactly comfy and relaxing. I hate to say it, but when she comes out with stuff like, "Make yourself at home!" it's a *little* bit phoney, considering she'll hyperventilate over crisp crumbs.)

"I just thought we needed to . . . freshen things up!" Mum had said with a nervous smile and a shrug, and a streak of Sugared Lilac in her hair.

She's asked me to live with the mental yellow for six months, and if I still hate it, I can change it. I've already picked out what I'm changing it to, which suits me so much more: Midnight Plum. Yes, it's dark, but if anyone can suggest something a little gloomier, I'd love to hear about it. . .

But back to headaches, since they are *such* fun.

I've had a particularly bad one today (Wednesday), because I had a horrible dream last night about swimming in the browny soup of the canal and cracking my head on a sunken shopping trolley.

Then I woke up and realized I'd smacked my forehead on the metal bar surrounding my delightful, luxury top-floor bunk.

"And for my project, this is what I have wrote—"

"Written," I correct Stan, as I trudge behind him and Alice B. Lovely and wonder if we have any ibuprofen at home. But Mum's been pretty rubbish at buying regular, essential sort of things since she got her great new job and her brilliant new marriage break-up, so I expect not.

"So what *have* you written?" Alice B. Lovely asks Stan encouragingly.

Mum and Dad had a big old phone fight about her last night. It went on for ever. It even went on after Stan was asleep, and considering Stan finds it hard to get to sleep at Dad's, that's really saying something.

Since we were staying at Dad's, I could only hear *his* side of the argument, of course, which went along the lines of how could Mum employ such an irresponsible idiot teenager to look after me and Stan (that's the highly edited version, of course).

Whatever Mum had said stayed a mystery. Except it must have been something along the lines of "I like her!" (edited version again), 'cause *there* was Alice B. Lovely, waiting patiently at the school gates for me today, hand-in-hand with a beaming Stanley.

And today Alice B. Lovely's outfit consisted of her furry-collared jacket, a tweedy pink mini kilt, sparkly gold tights and black patent T-bar shoes.

"Oh, jeez!" said Holly King, as she and her friends passed her by.

"Oh, lovely!" says Alice B. Lovely now, as we amble home.

She's faking interest in the homework book Stan is holding up to show her.

Today's eyelashes have the deep bluey-green pearlescent gleam of peacock feathers, and they seem to flutter slightly as she squints at the squiggly handwriting and age-six version of spelling and makes no sense of it, obviously.

Sighing with impatience, I catch up with the two of them and pull the book out of her hand.

All abut crocdills

1) Crocdills are riptills.
2) Crocdills liv in Merica, Afrka, Stralia, Nindia and other plasses.
3) Crocdills are clevr and biteey.
4) Crocdills are not alagaters.

I quickly translate and hand it back. I can't help notice that today Alice B. Lovely's eyes are a deep, deep blue to match the lashes.

"That's fantastic, Stan!" says Alice B. Lovely.

Stan grins shyly.

"I've got to do a drawing or make a model to go with it."

"Oh, I'm good at art," says Alice B. Lovely. "Maybe I can help you do it?"

"Oh, yes, please!" Stan practically burbles.

Humph.

I was going to help him with that.

We might have a matching pair of artistic designer parents, but let's face it, they certainly weren't going to have time to work on his project with him. So shouldn't that be a job for a big sister? Not a brand new who-does-she-think-she-is nanny!

And what's she going to help him make, anyway? Knowing *her* take on style, it'll probably be a Lego croc accessorized with a squirrel tail, hummingbird wings and sequinned beanie.

Actually, you know something? That's *it*.

Time is *up* for Alice B. Lovely.

I need to work out ways to get rid of this weird creature.

I found the weak spots in all the other nannies and I'll find hers too, I prom—

"Actually, I've just thought of something I want to show you." Alice B. Lovely interrupts my silent plotting. "Come on, let's cross the road here."

"Let's not," I mumble under my breath, but there's not much I can do apart from follow behind her and Stan. I'd hoped to hang out round at Tash's today, but she's had to go to the dentist. (I offered to go too, but her mum just looked at me funny. She has *no* idea just how dull and irritating my life is and how exciting a friend's dental appointment is by comparison.)

"What do you want to show us?" Stan says eagerly.

"Some *art*," beams Alice B. Lovely, taking his

hand and running around the corner, along the road, and into an alleyway.

By the time I catch them up (I didn't run; I *hate* running and I didn't want to look all desperate and keen), they are standing still and panting – and staring down at a paving stone.

I'm sorry . . . what could be so interesting about a *paving* stone?

"Edie! Look at this!" Stan calls out, getting down on his hands and knees.

Alice B. Lovely is tucking her curtains of hair behind her ears and crouching down beside him. "Check out this chewing gum, Edie!"

Excuse me? We're examining *litter*? I immediately think of nanny-number-whatever Cheryl passing by, casually spitting her gum after sneck-sneck-snecking it to death.

Thanks, but I'd rather be home reading my book, actu—

Oh!

It's a dried blob of gum . . . with a tiny *painting* on it.

Yuck! Why would someone paint on old gum?!

But hey, I guess I'm mildly curious, so I kneel down beside Stan to see better.

"A kitten! A little curled up kitten!" Stan says in delight.

"Don't you just love it?" says Alice B. Lovely. "Just think; someone stupid and irresponsible has spat out their chewing gum. And then ta-da! – another person comes along when it's all dried out and stuck to the pavement and turns it into actual *art*."

"Ta-da!"? Did she really just say something that *twee*? I wonder to myself.

"Come on; there's another one in the next street." Alice B. Lovely announces, scrabbling to her patent feet and holding out her hand for Stan.

And so we set off on a bizarre guided tour, me always a few reluctant steps behind Stan and Alice B. Lovely as they hurry on to the next piece of gum.

On our trail we see a miniature footballer, a vase of flowers, a map of Britain, an Easter chick, a Christmas tree, a guitar and a message that says, *Will you marry me, Dee? Love, Sam.*

"There are *two* to see here!" Alice B. Lovely calls out, leading us towards a parade of shops.

She and Stan stop and look down at something outside a charity shop. As I catch up with them, Alice B. Lovely glances up at me and points at a patch of pavement right where I'm about to step.

I crouch down on the pavement . . . and gasp.

I'm looking at a perfect, dainty clock face, painted on to an imperfect circle of dried-up old chewing gum.

The smaller of the feathery black hands is pointing to twelve, while the longer one is *just* about to catch up with it.

Around the edge of the clock face, there's some spidery, swirly writing.

It reads: *Countdown to happiness!*

Shivers of shock ripple through me.

(It's good that I'm kneeling down, otherwise I might just fall over.)

So . . . the happiness clock is real.

Tiny.

Made of gum.

But real.

And there I was, thinking it was just some nuts idea that existed in the privacy of my head.

(The blood pounds in my ears like a demented tick-tock.)

Why have I found this?

What is it trying to tell me?

Is it some kind of clue?

A message?

Wouldn't it be funny if it was trying to let me

know that it was time for my stupid, spiky-edged life to change?

"Edie! Edie! Come and look at *this* one," Stan calls out, waving me over.

As quickly as the thrill rushed over me, it ebbs away again.

I'm being stupid. *Way* too dramatic.

It's just a random coincidence, this dumb bit of gum art – not some magical sign that everything's going to be fantastic.

Face it; stuff like that does *not* happen in my grey little life.

Shaking the unexpected, unexplained ripples away, I stand up and walk over towards my brother.

Because Stan's hunched over and because of his shadow I can't see what he's peering at at first. Before I get the chance to look, I'm asked a question.

"So, do you like them?" says Alice B. Lovely, fixing her cobalt-blue eyes on me.

"Well, yeah," I have to admit. "How does someone come up with an idea so . . . pointless, though?"

"Well, it's not *really* pointless, is it?" says Alice B. Lovely. "The artist told me she likes the idea of taking something ugly and discarded and turning it into something small and beautiful."

"Hold on . . . you *know* her? The artist, I mean?" I say with a frown, trying to imagine the person who drew my happiness clock.

I mean, the cute little gum clock.

(*It has nothing to do with me*, I remind myself sternly.)

"Uh-huh," nods Alice B. Lovely. "She's my aunt."

"*Really?*"

It seems amazing that people would be related to a proper artist. A bit like someone being related to a premier footballer or a ballerina. It's so exotic.

"Yes, really!" laughs Alice B. Lovely. "What's so weird about that? *Your* mum and dad are artists."

I wouldn't say *that*. Mum designs dull clothes for dull women and Dad does websites that are for businesses called things like "Vans4Hire" and "Gary's Plumbing Supplies". My parents aren't doing anything that's likely to get hung in a gallery in my lifetime.

"Hey!" Stan suddenly squeaks. "Alice B. Lovely! Look!"

"You can just call me Alice," she laughs, making her silky curtains of hair ripple.

"Edie." Stan says urgently, realizing I'm there. "Look – this one's HER!"

He's staring up at Alice B. Lovely and pointing down at the mini-masterpiece.

I lean over and see a doll face peering back at me, with that familiar curtain of hair and eyes rimmed with feathery black lashes. Around the edge in swirly gold lettering, it spells out her name.

"It's not as pretty as the *real* you." Stan says, gazing from the gum to the human to the gum again.

"Aw, thanks, Stan." says Alice B. Lovely, smiling. "My aunt did that not so long ago."

But her smile's a little wobbly around the edges, I notice.

Why's that?

I should ask.

It's maybe the opportunity I've been looking for. If I can find out what's bugging her, perhaps I can torture her about it.

"Do you think she could do one of *me*?" Stan asks hopefully.

"Uh, I'm not sure," Alice B. Lovely says hesitantly. "It's complicated."

Yesss! Here we go. . .

"Complicated how?" I ask, all innocence.

"Just complicated," she shrugs, making her fluffy collar rise up and down behind her head.

"Any reason in particular?" I try again.

Stan is staring at me. He knows what I'm doing. He's seen me in action plenty of times before.

"Just complicated," Alice B. Lovely answers with a sweet smile, which of course is NOT the reaction I want.

Time to try something else I've just thought of.

"By the way, did you know that eighty-nine per cent of people who wear coloured contact lenses suffer from infections of the iris?"

It sounds like an excellent made-up condition, which I'm proud to say I just invented right this second. I haven't lost my touch. . .

"Edie, *don't*," says Stan, appearing in front of me, his hands on his hips.

Edie, don't.

Stan has never said that before in his life, unless it's to stop me from tickling him mercilessly or yanking the tap away from him when we both want a drink.

And he's never said it without a laugh in his voice or a grin on his face.

Right now, his Malteser eyes are serious and begging.

It's like they're asking me not to torture

Alice B. Lovely.

He can't *seriously* want her around, can he?

For the first time today, I feel like running.

So I run, run, run away from Alice B. Lovely with my head pound, pound, pounding as loud as the ticking of Nana's old clock of doom in the middle of the night. . .

Chapter 9

Rainbow Tinted Blues

Alice B. Quiet.

Alice B. Real.

Alice B. Gone.

It's Thursday afternoon and I'm sitting on a park bench, letting my mind buzz over alternative names for the girl who's getting on my nerves. The girl who Stan seems to be choosing over me.

(Alice B. Tween.)

"Come on, Max!" Tash is calling out beside me. "Good boy – bring me the toy!"

The puppy galumphs over with a chew toy in its mouth. I think it was once a plastic hedgehog but it's been gnawed so much it's hard to tell.

As Tash reaches out for the toy, Max shakes his head madly, sending trails of slobber flying. Some stick to my knees. Hanging out in the park after school today is better than hanging out with Alice B. Lovely, I know, but, well, *yuck* to slobbers.

By the way, I managed to avoid her for the rest of yesterday. Alice B. Lovely, I mean. I managed to avoid *everyone.* Mum might not trust me to look after myself, but at least she lets me have a key. So I ran, ran, ran back home, past a curious Mrs Kosma and her cluster of overfed pigeons and locked myself in my room – after scribbling and taping a note on the door that read: *Migraine: sleeping. Please leave me ALONE.*

They'd come knocking, of course. First Alice B. Lovely, then Stan, then Mum once she came home.

I grumbled about them disturbing me, and they left me alone, except Mum, of course. As soon as I'd seen the door handle turn and heard her voice asking to come in, I'd flicked the light off to send the room from custard yellow into darkness, and hoped she wouldn't spot the empty wrappers from my EMRGIZEE CHOCLIT stash.

"All right, sweetie?" she'd asked, feeling in the gloom for my forehead.

"No, I'm allergic to the latest nanny," I wanted to growl.

"My head hurts. I just need to be by myself," I said instead. "I'll be fine by morning."

She'd insisted on getting me a cool cloth and a glass of water so big it could have doubled as a vase, and then left me in peace.

And then went on to hang out with Alice B. Lovely, as I could hear when I jammed my ear up against the door.

Above the irritating tick-tocking of the clock of doom, I listened to what they were saying.

"The designs I'm working on?" Mum giggled, all giddy and shy-sounding. "Well, if you're *sure* you want to see them, I'll get my laptop out. . ."

"I really like the name 'Indigo Dove'," said Alice B. Lovely, obviously sucking right up to Mum.

"Well, I think the company chose it because most of our clothes are navy coloured. The 'Dove' part just sounds nice; it doesn't mean anything."

"Oh, but there *is* such a thing as an Indigo Dove. It's a South American bird."

"Really?" Mum said, all interested. (I bet Alice B. Lovely made that up, just to impress her. As a fact inventor myself, I can always spot another one a mile off.)

"What's the klective nine for 'doves'?" I heard Stan

ask, and Mum and Alice B. Lovely laughed, and Alice B. Lovely's laugh sounded a bit like a harp was being strummed in the living room and I wanted to *scream*.

Instead I stopped listening to all the cosiness and fun and whatever the collective noun was for stupid doves, and went back to the stress snack box.

You know, I'd had enough of hearing two-thirds of my family go gushy over this screwball girl. It was as if she was casting some sort of spell over Mum and Stan.

(Alice B. Witch.)

"Drop it! *Drop* it, Max. Good boy!" trills Tash. "What a mess – it's all chewed. We'll need to get you a *new* toy, won't we?"

"How about that dumb grey thing you keep on your bed?" I suggest, thinking of the fluffy bear I always tease her about. I just don't get how you can expect adults to treat you as all grown-up if you still keep a cuddly-wuddly for huggles at beddy-weddy time.

"Don't be *mean*, Edie," Tash frowns at me, and immediately turns back to Max, full of smiles and kisses for the tip of his damp, smelly nose.

I suddenly get the feeling that my supposed best

friend has been paying more attention to her dribbly dog than what I've just been telling her about yesterday.

"Hey, have you been listening to *anything* I've been saying?" I check with her.

Tash's face falls again.

"*Yes!*" she says defensively.

Uh-oh. I've annoyed her. But I guess I'm feeling so left out at home, the last thing I need is to have my best friend prefer her cute but dopey puppy to me. . .

"Alice B. Lovely liked your mum's designs and she's promised to help Stan build a life-sized crocodile out of wire and papier maché for his school project and it's making you cross. Did I get that right?"

When she says it back like that, it makes me seem stupid.

"It's a *bit* more complicated than that," I mutter, knowing my cheeks have flushed rosy red. I'd thought it would be great to hang out with her today after school in the park, but maybe she's as bad as the others. Suddenly I wish I could see Dad. He's the only one that hasn't been won over by Alice B. Lovely's sugary sweetness and dazzled by those batting (false) eyelashes.

"Sorry, Edie!" says Tash, leaning over to give me a hug. "Just don't give me a hard time, OK? I *am* on your side, remember?"

I relax a bit with gratitude, and then realize it's a mistake. The minute I do that, I have a bad habit of crying.

"Ice cream?" I ask brightly, blinking hard so the tears don't stand a chance.

I quickly stand up and attempt not to trip over Max, who's tangling up my legs like a dog-shaped rope.

"Sure. Strawberry, with sprinkles!" says Tash with one of her sunshiney smiles, as she grabs Max before he can follow me into the park café. "Hey, I forgot to ask – what's happening at the weekend?"

"Dunno," I say, walking backwards. She's talking about Mum and Dad, and their clashing plans to go away to work conferences/pitches/whatever. "One of them is going to have to back down, but I don't know which."

And I don't want to hear that argument, I think, as I turn and take the two steps that lead up to the café entrance.

Late last night, when I'd snuck out of my room to

the loo, I'd heard Mum on the phone to Nana, trying to get her to come down to stay with us on Saturday, but it sounded like the answer had been along the lines of "Well, no". It's not that Nana wouldn't have wanted to, but it hasn't been long since she had her hip replacement, so what was Mum thinking of? (Nothing, except her work.)

With a leaden heart I walk into the crowded park café, where I'm instantly hit with a wall of chatter and a too-loud radio. Some DJ is shouting that "it's time for a time-check; and it's coming up to five o'clock on this beee-*yoootiful* Thursday afternoon" over the top of a thumping dance track.

I feel like shouting, "Oh, shut up!" right back at him, but then the entire café full of people might think I was completely crazy, not just mildly grouchy.

"Mine!"

"No, *mine*."

"No, mine!"

"*I* saw it first."

"I *touched* it first!"

I hover for a second by the fridge, as two little kids argue and snarl over the last white chocolate Magnum.

"Yours!"

"No, *yours*."

"No, yours, definitely!"

As I wait, I tune into the similar-but-different conversation going on in the booth to the side of me.

"No, yours are *definitely* the most gorgeous, Dionne."

Dionne?

I turn my head a fraction and see three beautiful, flicky-haired girls, busy comparing their hands. Cara and Holly have obviously copied Dionne and gone for the alien lobster claw makeover.

"Do you think so?" says Dionne, holding her square-edged talons up to the light streaming through from the big plate-glass windows.

Linzee (nanny number four or five) used to regularly hold her nails up to admire their fake (un) loveliness. I always enjoyed watching her struggling to make our tea; she'd open jars and chop vegetables with all the ease of a crab trying to open a packet of crisps. The more I stared in wonder, the more it would wind her up, of course, till those claws began rap-rap-rapping on the chopping board.

"OMG. . ." drawls Dionne.

Wow. Is she *that* impressed with her own manicure?

"Junk Shop Girl is looking her junkiest *yet*!"

Even though I'm getting an Arctic blast from the open freezer, I feel a hot flush rush over me, as I instinctively know who Dionne's talking about.

"That is *so* bad," mutters Cara, staring out towards the not-too-far-away trees.

"*Totally* bad," agrees Holly.

I'm holding my breath, as though that'll help me turn invisible, or stop Dionne, Cara and Holly from turning around and seeing me there.

And as my heart thumps overheated blood around my body, I check out Alice B. Lovely for myself.

Against the brown and green of the trees, her red polka-dot skirt stands out like she's wearing a tablecloth. And today she's mismatched her battered gold shoes with little-girl white ankle socks.

She's *way* too far away for me to see what colour her eyes (and eyelashes) are, but I *can* see she's staring up into the trees, along with Stan. They are both slowly turning around, like ballerinas on top of a music box. They are both holding things. What *are* they up to?

"Who's the kid?" I hear Cara wonder aloud.

"Think he's the little brother of that sulky Year-Eight girl," says Holly.

My temperature suddenly spikes so high I might blow the top off a thermometer, if anyone dared to stick one in my mouth just now.

"Oh, yeah," laughs Dionne. "The one who always looks like she's up for a fight!"

I'm suddenly shaking, and feeling slightly sick.

Is that *really* how they see me?!

"HEY, EXCUSE ME, MISS! CAN YOU SLIDE THAT LID CLOSED?" booms a voice from behind the counter. "YOU'RE LETTING ALL THE COLD AIR OUT!"

The "miss" is me.

The kids who were fighting over the white chocolate Magnum are gone.

The lid of the freezer is open, with a mist of icy air rising up.

Everyone in the café is idly looking to see who's being shouted at, including Dionne, Cara and Holly.

I want to curl up and die.

"It's *her*," I vaguely hear one of the sixth formers say.

I clearly hear the sniggering that goes with it, as me and my sulky face rush right out of the café.

"What? What's up?" asks Tash, as I hurriedly approach the bench where she's waiting.

"Can we just go? *Now?*" I say, heading straight for the path that'll lead us to the nearest park exit.

I want to be a million miles away from those girls, from Alice B. Lovely, and even from Stan right now.

"Sure, but what's wrong?" asks Tash, jumping up to join me. "Has something happ— Max! Max, come back!"

But Max isn't coming back.

Max is lolloping off in the direction of someone he knows, barking his hellos.

"Max!" Stan calls out, distracted from his slow-motion pirouetting and skyward staring.

Naturally, he bends down to cuddle the puppy, and naturally he looks round for Tash, and naturally he spots me.

"Edie! Hey, Edie – come see this!"

What do I do? Run again?

I don't know if I could do that to Stan. He was a bit clingy with me at breakfast time, hanging on my arm, like he'd missed me, or was worried about me. (It made it quite hard to cut up my beans on toast.)

So I guess there's no choice but to head over.

And as I do, I can feel three sets of mocking, curious eyes following me from the café. (Ugh. . .)

"Hello!" smiles Alice B. Lovely.

"What were you looking at?" I ask Stan, ignoring that hello and the amber eyes staring at me. I think the eyelashes are rainbow tinged, but I'm not going to look again to check.

"Hi," says Tash. (Traitor.)

"The dancing spiders!" says Stan, his freckly face full of wonder.

He's still petting Max with one hand, but pointing upwards with the other. Max is sniffing the thing that Stan's been holding, and I see that it's Arthur, come for a walk in the park.

I gaze up warily, not sure what exactly I'm going to see, and not very keen to look, to be honest.

Nothing. I can see nothing but branches and leaves and dappled sunlight.

"Where?" asks Tash, squinting like me at the invisible dancing spiders.

"Look for the tiny strings of web – they twinkle in the light!" says Alice B. Lovely.

Sure enough, one second there's clear air, and next there are dozens and dozens – maybe even hundreds – of tiny, pinhead-sized spiders dangling from rainbow-coloured threads of webbing. It's maybe one of the strangest things I've ever seen. Not counting Alice B. Lovely.

"It happens on these types of trees at this time of year," Alice B. Lovely. "Everyone passes underneath, without realizing this is going on right above their heads."

I want to ask her how she knows, but don't want to seem too interested. Luckily, Tash does it for me.

"How did you find out about them?" says my best friend.

"My dad . . . he's a park ranger," she explains. "He—"

Her mobile springs to life, with a jangle like sleigh bells. It makes me look her way properly. I see that *she's* holding a bent-eared, battered pink bunny. Of *course* she'd be one of those soft-toy-on-the-bed girls. Did she take it along today to "bond" with Stan and Arthur? Very cunning. Very phoney.

"Hello?"

As Alice meanders off a few steps to talk to whoever, Stan jumps to his feet and comes to hug me, walloping Arthur into the small of my back.

Actually, I have to admit that it's the best thing that's happened to me all day, and I hug him back.

Gazing down into his freckly face, I feel the bad stuff fade away.

Who cares about the girls back in the café? Who cares what they think of me? How can I trust the judgement of people who think having weird coloured claws for nails is cool?

"Edie?" says Stan, blinking those Malteser eyes at me.

"Yes, buddy?" I manage to smile for the first time in what feels like a long time.

"Isn't Alice B. Lovely . . . like *magic*?"

As my heart sinks, the "magical" Alice B. Lovely is holding out her phone to me.

"It's Justine. I mean, your mum," she says, batting her eyelashes. (They really do match the rainbow threads of the mid-air spider web.)

"Mum?" I say warily. "Are you all right?"

"Of course!" her faraway voice laughs. "I just wanted to check that YOU were all right. No headaches today?"

"Yeah, I'm fine," I mumble.

I'm crushed, mortified, jealous and a little bit miserable but fine. What's new?

"Oh, good!" Mum sighs with relief. "I was a little worried about you last night."

Yeah. *So* worried that she chatted away happily to Alice B. Lovely for at least half an hour after she'd checked on me. (And what was with Alice B. Lovely? Didn't she have a home to go to?)

"But hey, listen – I just wanted to tell you," Mum continues, "I decided to ask Alice to mind you guys all day on Saturday, so me and your dad can both go to our work meetings. I won't be back till quite late . . . but that's OK, isn't it?"

I take a deep breath and let it out slowly.

"Yeah, it's OK," I finally mumble.

Of course in my *alternative* dictionary, "OK" means "more awful than I can put into words".

You know, in this particular pocket of time, I *might* just be the most unhappy I've been since the day Dad moved out.

Oh, yes, I have the blues.

The deep navy blues.

The indigo blues, even.

Or maybe they're rainbow-tinted blues.

But as I stand here mulling over the exact shade of my misery, my mind drifts to a tiny painting on a pavement not very far away.

Oh, little clock of happiness . . . if only you were real, and not just a doodle on a dried-up, scuzzy blob of gum.

Chapter 10

Pop Goes the Gladness Bubble

Oh joy, oh joy, oh joy.

And I mean that in a one hundred per cent sarcasm-free way.

'Cause there is no Junk Shop Girl waiting to meet me today at the gate. In amongst a huddle of mums is a handsome man. He has scruffy but cool hair, and is wearing a scruffy but cool jacket, T-shirt and jeans. If it wasn't for a trace of grey in his sideburns, he might pass – at a distance like this – for my big brother.

I'm so relieved, and so glad, glad, *glad*.

My heart was somewhere in the basement when I came out of after-school club a second ago, mainly 'cause I'd spotted Dionne, Holly and Cara ambling out of the sixth-form block, and I don't have Tash for support today – she's at a follow-up dentist appointment.

Till I spotted Dad's welcome, warm smile I'd felt like I'd rather do DIY dentistry on myself with a Black & Decker drill than walk alone across the vast expanse of the playground without Tash for comfort (or armour).

"Hey, Edie-beady-bear!" he calls out as I hurry towards him.

Ouch. That *does* bump my fragile bubble of gladness a bit, but I'll forgive him, because I'm SO pleased . . .

a) to see him, and . . .
b) that he's not Alice B. Lovely.

"What are you doing here?" I ask, waves of, well, *joy* burbling in my chest.

"Thought I'd surprise you and take you out for a pizza, if that's all right."

"Yeah, that's pretty much all right!" I laugh, as Dad loops his arm around my shoulders and gives me a squeeze. (For thirteen years, I've never liked pizza, 'cause of the cheese. Dad should know this, but in the circumstances, I'm not going to make a big deal of it.)

I wonder what's going on? Maybe after thinking

Stan was about to hurtle over the edge of his balcony earlier in the week, Dad has had a wake-up call. Maybe he's decided to rejig his work schedule and give up on someone else looking after us on *his* days. Maybe he's planning to meet me and Stan from school every Tuesday and Friday for ever and ever from now on. Maybe—

Wait a minute. . .

"Where's Stan?" I ask, glancing around.

"Alice has picked him up," he says brightly.

I wonder if he feels me jerk with disappointment.

"And where are they?" I ask, holding on to the possibility of the pizza treat being one of those daddy-and-daughter things.

"They're going to meet us at the pizza restaurant."

Great.

And I mean that with one hundred per cent sarcasm.

(*Pop!* goes my gladness bubble. . .)

"What's that sigh for, Edie-beady-bear?"

Oh. Did I do that out loud? I didn't realize I had. But perhaps it's a chance for me to make sure Dad is on my side.

"I dunno," I say wearily. "I'm just not sure about her. . ."

"Alice?" Dad checks.

It feels weird when he says it like that. I never, ever think of her as just plain "Alice". It somehow doesn't sound like the same person. I mean, to her face I call her . . . actually, I've never called her anything. Mainly 'cause I've tried to talk to her as little as possible so far this week.

"Yes, *her*," I say, taking the latest opportunity not to say her name out loud. "Did you know that Mum's got her looking after us tomorrow? All day? Into the *evening*?"

"Yes, she told me. And to be honest, Edie-beady-bear, I'm not that happy about it," Dad says solemnly.

(Yessss!)

"In fact, that's why I ducked out of work early tonight, and why I thought we should have tea together. I know your mum said the balcony thing was all a misunderstanding, but you know what Justine's like – she thinks she knows *everything*. Oh, sorry, Edie, didn't mean to say that. I, er, just meant, I'm still not totally reassured."

(Yessss! Even *with* him letting a Mum grumble slip out.)

"And frankly, if this Alice girl doesn't convince

me tonight, then I'm going to blow out this work meeting tomorrow and let Eric go on his own."

(Yessss! Yessss! *Yessss!*)

At last.

Things are FINALLY nudging my way.

". . .So *I* said 'How about we put a sun slowly rising behind your logo' and you should have *seen* our client's face. I knew right *then* that we'd got the job!"

"Wow, no wonder!" says Alice B. Lovely. "It looks amazing."

Noooooooooooo! I think to myself, as I doodle agitatedly on a serviette.

This *wasn't* supposed to happen. Dad *wasn't* supposed to fall for her, like the rest of my family had done.

But here he is, holding up his phone to show Alice B. Lovely some website design, and she's sparkling her sea-green eyes at whatever's on the screen. (Her eyes *are* literally sparkling; they're the same mini-mirrored false lashes she wore when we first met her on Monday.)

So when did Dad change from stern-and-concerned to chatty-and-matey? I'd like to say it took a long time for him to warm to Alice B. Lovely, but we haven't even *ordered* yet.

Here's how it happened:

- We got here.
- We said our hellos.
- Stan ran and sat on Dad's lap and told him that Alice B. Lovely was a real, true artist and that she'd just taken him to the hardware shop and that the strange roll of wire over by the coat rack was for the life-sized crocodile they were going to be starting on tomorrow.
- Dad melted.

And so they've started chatting like they're bestest friends, wittering on about art school (where Dad went, where Alice B. Lovely wants to go), about art they like (Dad's into 1950s prints, Alice B. Lovely "adores" installations, whatever they are).

Stan keeps chipping in, mentioning the gum art on the pavement (Dad's keen to see it) and how Alice B. Lovely is related to a real, true artist "what is her aunt".

"And is she lovely like you?" Dad asked a minute ago, and nearly made me barf.

(Except I stopped short, slightly stunned to see

that what I'd been doodling was a spidery version of the clock on the piece of gum outside the charity shop. I quickly scrunched it up.)

"No," I heard Alice B. Lovely answer with a laugh, getting Dad's "joke". "Her name is Maggie Baxter."

Dad said he'd Google her stuff. Alice B. Lovely looked chuffed.

And now she is acting as if Dad's website designs are a work of staggering genius and I've lost my appetite.

Which is unfortunate, because the waiter has just turned up.

"Would you like to order?" he asks, holding up his pad in one hand and picking up my scrunched serviette in the other.

"I'll have an Americano, please," says Dad, as Alice B. Lovely drops her glittering gaze to the menu. "What about you, buddy?"

"Margherita!" yelps Stan.

"Alice? What do *you* fancy?"

Hello? Am I last to be asked? Least important person at the table, etc.?

"I'll have a burger, please," I say quickly.

"One . . . cheeseburger. . ." the waiter mutters as he scribbles.

"No – just a *regular* burger. She doesn't like cheese," says Alice B. Lovely, blinking up at the waiter and temporarily blinding him, probably.

Irritation bubbles in my chest.

"Excuse me, but I *can* speak for myself," I tell her firmly.

Alice B. Lovely doesn't flinch.

She just stares at me with her big dolly eyes as if she's trying to figure me out.

She reminds me even more of that spooky, antique porcelain doll that used to be in Nana's china cabinet; when I was little I felt like its gaze followed me round the room, whether I was sitting hunched over a book or staring into space. (Yes, visits to Nana are action-packed.)

But hold on . . . pause those thoughts about Nana's old house.

What's this? Dad has just frowned at me!

Why am *I* in the wrong? Am I not allowed to speak?

"I'm going to the loo," I say, squeaking my chair back loudly.

"I'll come with you, Edie," says Stan, hurtling off Dad's knee and racing me to the door by the coat rack.

(I feel like kicking the roll of wire as I pass, but I'd only be putting a dent in Stan's fledgling crocodile.)

From the second we go into the toilets till the second we come out, Stan can't stop talking. No prizes for *who* he's talking about: Alice B. Lovely, of *course*.

"She came and picked me up early from after-school club!"

"And we bought that wire stuff in this really cool shop with big hammers and stuff!"

"And then we hung out at the park and played Tickle Tag, which is *just* like Tag only you have to *tickle* the person when you catch them!"

"And she lives on the other side of the park, and she can see a magpie nest from her bedroom window!"

"And she taught me a rhyme about magpies that goes, '*One for sorrow, two for joy...*'"

What was it with the bird stuff? Alice B. Lovely knows they stress him out!

And all Stan's chit-chat is stressing *me* out. I feel like sticking my head under the hand dryer so I can't hear any more.

But I guess the sooner I go back out there, the sooner we can eat and the sooner we can leave the restaurant AND Alice B. Lovely.

I don't like what I see when we walk over to the table, though.

Dad and Alice B. Lovely seem to be whispering and smiling, like they have some sort of secret.

"Hey, tiger!" says Dad. "Back so soon?"

"Grrrr!" Stan jokily growls his answer.

"What – didn't you *want* us to come back, Dad?" I ask, feeling flushes of hot and cold and anger and crushing hurt.

"Don't be silly, Edie-beady-bear!" Dad laughs, not even noticing that I might be a teeny bit mad or sad. "But guess what? I know something *you* don't!"

Dad and Alice B. Lovely grin at each other and then at us.

Great. They really *do* have a secret.

"What? What is it?" asks Stan, bouncing like a freckly Tigger.

"A-ha!" Dad says annoyingly. "You'll just have to wait till tomorrow, and Alice will reveal all."

That she's an evil sorceress in disguise, maybe? Come to steal my family away from me?

Maybe she wants to take my place. Push me out of the nest, like a magpie, or a cuckoo, or whatever stupid bird does that stuff.

"Not fair!" yelps Stan. "I want to know the secret NOW!"

Really?

Well, I want to know the secret *never*.

I reach into my bag, take out my book and start reading, not caring *how* rude I look.

As far as I'm concerned, the ruder the better. . .

Chapter 11

From Dull to Shiny (In Twelve Steps)

The start of my day has been a lot less than lovely. Here's why. . .

1) I sat up in bed this morning and whacked my head on the ceiling. (I forgot I was at Dad's, not Mum's.)
2) In the car on the way over to Mum's, Dad gave me a talking-to about my "attitude". (I'm acting very juvenile, *apparently*. Pretty funny coming from someone who threw a strop when his precious Arsenal mug got broken.)
3) Back at home (Mum's) I looked online ('cause Stan made me) and found out that Indigo Doves really *are* real and really *do* come from South America. Drat.

4) While she was getting ready to go to her conference, Mum went on about how she's had all these great, last-minute ideas to add colour accents and glitter to the Indigo Dove range. All thanks to being inspired by Alice Bogging Lovely, of *course*. . .

And now that the doorbell has just ding-donged, and Mum has left with hurried kisses for me and Stan, we're stuck for the day – the long, endless day – with you-know-who.

"Alice B. Lovely! Hurray! Ooohhhh!!"

Stan can do what he likes. He can cheer and "ooohhhh," for all I care.

Me? I've sulkily squished myself into a beanbag and I'm reading my book. My not-very-good vampire book.

"Wow!"

Arghhh! It's too hard to ignore Stan's enthusiasm completely, and I quickly glance up to see what all his fussing is about.

Right, so there's Alice B. Lovely standing in the living room doorway.

(So far, so whatever.)

She's wearing her swishy flamingo skirt and

clutching something, and this time it isn't a battered please-can-we-be-friends pink bunny. It's a box, and she's opening it.

When she spots my gaze, she blinks back at me, like a dog hoping for a hug, or a bit of leftover sausage.

Actually, Tash's puppy Max has that exact same expression plastered on his dopey, cute face when he's just done a wee in her wardrobe or somewhere *else* he knows he shouldn't have done one.

But I don't suppose Alice is in need of a hug or a sausage, and I'm pretty certain she hasn't peed in an inappropriate place.

She's staring at me because she's willing me to look at something.

And you know what? I'm not going to do it. I am *not* going to look.

I am going to slouch here on the beanbag and read my rotten book, and pretend I don't notice the blinking, *or* the fact that today's set of eyelashes are black and strangely jaggedy and her eyes are the colour of honey.

Where was I? I wonder, skimming through and quickly finding the turned-over corner. *Oh, yes: chapter 6, page 162*, I remind myself, ignoring the sudden tippetty-tappetty noises nearby, and the fact that my brother is gasping so much he can't even talk.

The scream was lodged in her throat, hard as a nutshell, as Jed leaned closer. . . I read. *If only she could believe he was about to kiss her, instead of revealing the fangs she suspected were only a glint away. If only—*

"Edie! Edie!!" Stan finally manages to squeak. "Look, Edie!!"

Gripping the book, I lift my head and glare at Stan.

"*Yes*, Stan," I say in my best seen-it-all voice. "I *can* see it, thank you."

Well, much as I'd like to, it *is* pretty hard to ignore a big, pointy-beaked black-and-white bird hopping around your living room.

"What is it?" yelps Stan, waving around a slice of peanut butter and toast that he hasn't finished eating.

"A magpie," says Alice B. Lovely, looking fondly at the thing that's now flapped on to the coffee table and started pecking at the remote control button. "Is that all right, Stan? Having him here, I mean?"

"I LOVE it!!" squeals Stan. "How come you've got it? Is it your pet?"

"Well, yes," says Alice B. Lovely, untying the belt of her furry jacket and revealing a long-sleeved top as honey-coloured as today's eyes. "My dad found him in the park at the beginning of the summer – he was only a couple of days old, so I hand-reared him."

What's Alice B. Lovely playing at? Who keeps a pet *magpie*, for goodness' sake?

"What's its name?" Stan garbles, kneeling down closer to check out the bird and then giggling madly as it pecks off a chunk of his toast.

"He's called Buddy."

"*Buddy!!*" Stan is so excited his squeak could burst eardrums. "That's what Dad calls *me*! Did you hear that, Edie?"

"Yep," I say flatly, keeping my eyes on the page and trying to ignore the fact that the bird has now hopped on to the floor beside me.

"I know you've been feeling funny about birds lately, so I spoke to your dad last night and asked if he thought it might be a good idea to introduce you to Buddy. Maybe help you feel more relaxed around birds."

What, is she *Dr* Alice B. Lovely now? It's like she's constantly trying to impress us.

And yeah, so it might be working with Stan, but he's a kid, and everyone knows they can be easily impressed by stuff like sweets, and, er, magpies. But not *me*. No way.

Back to my book. . .

If only she didn't believe he was about to put his soft mouth on her neck and cruelly pierce the warm skin th—

Tap.

Tap.

Scrabble, rustle . . . rustle, rustle. . .

Tap.

OK, OK, so the magpie doesn't seem to want to be ignored. Its beak is *right* in my book, and at the same time it's giving me the once-over with its searching little eyes.

"What's it doing?" I hear myself asking, as the bird burrows its beak somewhere between page 30 and page 50.

"He's caching," explains Alice B. Lovely, gazing on like a proud mum.

As explanations go, it's pretty lame, seeing as I don't have a clue what caching means.

"It's like a game of hide-and-seek," she says now, spotting my confusion. "Magpies love to tuck away their favourite finds and rediscover them about ten seconds later."

"So what's it trying to tuck away?" I ask, wondering if I dare peek, with that beak in pecking range of my fingers.

But yes, I have to admit that I *am* suddenly curious.

And kind of *charmed* by this hopping, head-tilting creature.

"Well, *toast*," says Alice, watching as her pet tap-taps the lumpy pages together firmly.

Hmm.

Peanut butter and vampires ... I'm not *entirely* sure that's a great combination.

I wave my hand to shoo the bird away. It stares at me with black beady eyes, and blinks these weird bright yellow inner eyelids at me, as if it's thinking about what to do. I have a feeling one of the options it's considering isn't being shooed.

What I'm *not* expecting is what comes out of its shiny black beak.

"Hello!"

Huh?

That was a squawking, scratchy sound, but it was definitely a word.

"It said hello!" I practically squawk myself.

"Yes!" laughs Alice B. Lovely, making her curtains of hair ripple and the double cherry on her long necklace sway.

"But – but only parrots can do that," I protest, while Stan jumps up and down on the spot clapping his hands and shouting, "He spoke! Buddy spoke!"

"Magpies can copy some basic sounds," Alice B. Lovely explains, kicking the door of the pet carrier box closed with the toe of her beat-up gold shoes. "They're not as sophisticated as birds in the parrot family, but they can do pretty good attempts at words."

Right on cue, Buddy hops on my knee and says, "Smile! Smile, sweetie! Smile!"

I can't help it; I don't just *smile*, I burst out laughing, and the unexpected sound of that shocks Stan enough to stop bouncing and Buddy enough to fly off.

"There are no windows open, are there?" Alice B. Lovely asks in a sudden panic, following Buddy's whack-whack-whack of wings out into the corridor.

"I don't know – maybe in the kitchen?" I fret, flinging down my toasted book and running after her.

"The thing is, Buddy doesn't fly free!" Alice B.

Lovely calls out, frantically looking into Mum's Frosted Lilac bedroom as she rushes by. "He's always either inside at our place or in his cage!"

In my hurry, my hip thwacks against the corner of the hall table.

Almost in slow motion, I see the clock of doom slip-slide off it and fall to the floor with an ominous clunk.

I've daydreamed about it breaking for so long, but now it's actually happening I feel sick.

Time lurches and speeds up fast again as my fingers curl around the cool wood and I lift it up.

I see with relief that the glass isn't smashed and the second hand is still moving.

Much as I hate the thing, what I'd hate more is for Nana's clock to be broken and for Mum to have yet *another* reason to be fed up with me, I realize, as I gingerly place it back on to the table.

"Don't worry! Buddy's here!" I hear Stan yelp.

Somehow my little brother has skedaddled to the kitchen before us and is standing panting by the sink.

Oh, thank goodness. There's the magpie, strutting up and down on the kitchen windowsill and staring down into the communal back garden.

"The window's open a *little* bit," I notice, "but it's OK – Mum's got it on the catch, so it won't open any wider."

"Hmm . . . he's not happy about something," says Alice B. Lovely, hurrying over to join her bird and Stan.

"What is it?" I ask, peering out. All I can see is washing on the line, Mrs Kosma's collection of flapping pirate-sail dresses.

"Oh, *I* know! It's because those clothes are all black – he thinks they're crows."

"Very *wide*, big crows!" I find myself laughing out loud for the second time today, thinking of wobbly Mrs Kosma, who RIGHT at that second appears from behind one of the dresses with what looks like a bag of old bread in her hand, ready to feed her pigeon friends.

She's looking up, frowning, trying to see the source of the laughing.

"Hello!" squawks Buddy at top volume.

Mrs Kosma frowns at the sight of three human faces and a strutting bird on the *inside* of the window ledge.

"Smile, sweetie! Smile!" Buddy squawks some more.

Mrs Kosma takes a step back in surprise.

"*Pppffffffffffffftt!!*" I snort loudly, then have to step away, slapping my hands across my mouth.

She must think it's one of us being cheeky. But what can we do? I can hardly open the window and explain we have a tame pet talking magpie in here, or the tame pet talking magpie might fly away.

Alice B. Lovely gives a little whistle and pats Stan's left shoulder – and Buddy obediently flaps right on to it.

"Can you take him back through to the living room?"

Stan nods and heads off, and Alice B. Lovely whips her phone out of a pocket in her flamingo skirt.

"What are you doing?" I ask, as she holds it to her eyes and clicks.

"I've got to take a photo of those dresses before your neighbour takes them down," she answers.

"Why? What's so interesting about old lady dresses?"

"They just look kind of beautiful and weird. Like a cloud of black kites, or. . ."

"Or sails on a pirate ship?" I suggest.

"Yes, they do a bit," says Alice B. Lovely, blinking

her jaggedy black lashes. "It's like they're like a great piece of installation art."

"What *is* installation art?" I ask.

I've never wanted to seem interested in anything Alice B. Lovely's had to say before, but now it's like I've forgotten to care whether I show it or not.

"Um . . . unexpected art, I guess," she replies. "Like at the South Bank, there was a giant urban fox – as big as a building – made out of straw. Or at the gallery in town, I once saw a flock of seagulls, only they were just paper planes, suspended on wires!"

Her face has gone all dreamy, the way Tash's does when she mentions Max, or Stan's does when you get him talking about Lego.

And I get the chance to look more closely at her eyelashes for the first time, and they're a work of art themselves. They must be made out of two tiny, thin strips of fine plastic, and are miniature scenes of grass, flowers and butterflies. They're like the detailed black silhouette illustrations in a Cinderella book I used to love when I was little. (Where was that now? Probably packed away at the back of the cupboard with the stupid safari hippo and all my other babyish stuff.)

"And then there's this really famous artist who once made hundreds of frozen mini men," Alice B. Lovely babbles on. "He put them on some steps, till they melted."

"What's the point of that?" I frown. "Why would you spend ages making something if it disappears as soon as the sun comes out?"

"Well, he filmed it, of course!" says Alice B. Lovely, with one of her harp-in-the-room laughs. "And *that* becomes the art. *That's* what can be shown in galleries."

I'm still frowning, uncertain.

"You liked Maggie Baxter's stuff, didn't you?" she checks with me.

"Your aunt's stuff? The chewing gum?" I say. "Yeah. It's cute."

"And it won't last for ever. People will walk on them, and they'll wear away. But she photographs each one as she does it, so it's preserved that way."

I feel my frown fading and my eyebrows raising. I look intrigued, I know I do, and Alice B. Lovely spots that and takes advantage straightaway.

"Get your jacket on – I want to show you something," she says in a soft voice, but one that's giving me an order, for sure.

"What about your bird, though?" I ask.

"Leave him with the toast, and he'll have fun," she says brightly. "We can clear up the caching later. . ."

Stan and Alice B. Lovely are too fast for me.

I'm running, focusing on the blur of his bright blue Converse trainers and her gold beat-up 1920s shoes.

By the time I catch up with them, they are staring at an ad on the side of a bus shelter and giggling.

Why is an ad for perfume so funny? I've seen this one before: some impossibly pretty girl sulking attractively while holding up a bottle of something expensively smelly.

"Edie, look!" says Stan pointing at the model's face.

Ah, she's not quite sulking any more. Someone has drawn a smiling mouth full of teeth and braces and plastered it on top of her pout.

Yeah, that's pretty funny.

"Next one!" says Alice B. Lovely, and we're off again, to a bus shelter just down the road.

This time, we're stopping to stare at an oily-chested hunk who's advertising men's deodorant.

His chiselled good looks are ruined a bit by the huge googly cross-eyes someone has stuck on his face.

I burst out laughing, which seems to please Stan and Alice B. Lovely no end.

"I did do more, but they've been taken down already," says our childminder, holding her phone up and clicking through some images on the screen.

Ah, *I* get it. Alice B. Lovely did this stuff.

"Is *this* installation art?" I ask, as I look at snaps of a toothpaste ad featuring a grinning model with blacked-out teeth; a car ad with giant eyelashes fixed to the headlights; and Kate Moss with a moustache. (Seeing one of the most iconic faces ever with facial fuzziness makes me snort out loud again. What is *with* me and all this snorting today?)

"Yes!" says Alice B. Lovely, enthusiastically. "Either of *you* fancy having a go?"

With the hand that isn't holding her phone, she's rifling in her bag and pulling out a clear plastic folder filled with what looks like a stash of white paper, some pens and a pair of scissors.

"Yes, yes, *yes*!" Stan yelps, doing his Tigger bounces on the spot.

Before I know what's happening, Stan has run

around to the far side of the bus shelter and drawn a speech bubble that says, "Boo!"

"Excellent!" announces Alice B. Lovely, handing a blob of Blu-tack to my brother.

"But isn't this like graffiti? Couldn't we get into trouble?" I ask, as Stan fixes his "Boo" to the mouth of a perky Jack Russell in a dog food ad.

Alice B. Lovely twirls her head around to look at me, her hair swishing like a swoop of silk.

"Don't worry – I use Blu-tack to put these bits of artwork up, so I'm not technically *damaging* anything," Alice B. Lovely answers, holding her phone up to her face. "And I take them down as soon as I've got a photo of the ad."

She pauses and snaps Stan's first ever attempt at installation art.

"But . . . but you haven't taken down *any* of the ones you've just shown us," I point out.

Alice B. Lovely blinks at me from behind her phone.

"Um, well, *sometimes* it's fun to leave them up for a little while, just to make people laugh!" she says with a sweet grin.

"Which means we *could* get caught and we *could* get into trouble?" I suggest, nibbling at my lip.

"Of course not," Alice B. Lovely reassures me, though she's looking a little nervous around the edges herself. "Well, what I mean is, we'll *never* get caught . . . if we *run*!"

Oh, *boy* – with that, we run and we run, from bus shelter to bus shelter, only stopping when. . .

a) Stan plasters random "Boo!"s on posters (the baby in the talc ad, a banana in a supermarket ad and a Highland cow advertising holidays in Scotland), and . . .
b) we're laughing too much to run.

"Come on, it's *your* turn, Edie!" Stan says, handing me a marker pen and a challenge.

We've now arrived at the other side of the high street, and we're in between the town hall and the art gallery. I'm feeling high on adrenaline after all that running.

I'm also feeling stupidly nervous. There are people milling about, paying us no attention. But what happens if they see me doing something to the bus stop? Will they think I'm vandalizing it?

"Come on, Edie! Have a go!" urges Alice B. Lovely.

So I glance at the ad on the side of the shelter (it

features a cute little kid holding a glass of milk) and come up with an idea.

Scribble, scribble, scribble.

Snip, snip, snip.

"Here, Edie," says Alice B. Lovely, passing me a blob of Blu-tack.

The cheeks of her pale doll face are pink and her fairy-tale eyes are wide. She is radiating encouragement.

"Hey, look – there's a bus coming!" squeals Stan.

Stick, stick, stick.

CLICK! and Alice B. Lovely has captured my artwork for posterity.

"Edie, quick – get back over here," she says, urging me to follow her.

We sprint to the nearest wall, beside a glass-fronted noticeboard flagging up what's on at the art gallery.

With my heart beating, I pretend to read the info, while Alice B. Lovely and Stan lean back casually and watch for reactions from the passengers on the bus.

"Aww," says Stan, sounding disappointed. "It's not very busy!"

"Apart from those three girls on the top deck,"

says Alice B. Lovely. "*They're* looking pretty freaked."

"They're big girls from your school, aren't they, Edie?" Stan points out.

OK, so thumping heart or not, I have to look now.

And I burst out laughing again, as I recognize Dionne, Cara and Holly, who are all frowning at side of the bus shelter in total confusion. 'Cause instead of an ad for milky goodness, they see a kid with fangs, drinking a glass of something I've just coloured in red. (At least the rubbish vampire book's been good for *something*. Apart from caching, of course.)

Still, I don't want them to spot *me* spotting *them* (there's nothing like the dead-eyed stares of mean girls to flat line your mood) so I spin around again and carry on pretending to study the notices in the art gallery board.

Alice B. Lovely is doing the same.

"Look!" Alice B. Lovely gasps, tapping the glass with one finger.

Oh – maybe she's *not* pretending.

"'Art Under . . . feet'," Stan reads hesitantly from the poster.

"'Art Underfoot'," I correct him, as I read it too.

"'An exhibition of the unique works of—'"

"Alice B. Lovely – it's your auntie! It's *your auntie!!*" he gabbles.

He's right. It's a show of Maggie Baxter's mad but amazing gum art. Photos of every one of them are going to be displayed here from next weekend.

I find myself laughing with surprise at the coincidence.

Stan's reaction is to jump up and down, of course.

And what about Alice B. Lovely?

She turns to us with her incredibly crazy, incredibly beautiful eyes, which seem more enormous with wonder than ever.

Instinctively, I grab my phone from my pocket, flick to the camera option with my thumb, point it straight at Alice B. Lovely and CLICK!, I have a piece of artwork of my own. . .

"I think he's *finally* asleep," says Alice B. Lovely, tiptoeing back from Stan's room and flopping down on the sofa beside me.

She'd gone back in with Arthur the crocodile. Her magpie had taken such a shine to Arthur, snuggling up and nudging him, that Stan had said Arthur could stay up late and play with Buddy.

But then as time wore on, Stan sort of lost it, and cried for Arthur. It was no wonder he was beside himself, I guess; there's only so much wild pet birds, illegal art, vegetable-monster-making and full-size crocodile modelling a small boy can take before his brain explodes with over-stimulation.

"Good, he's exhausted," I say, gently stroking the head of Buddy, who's now roosting on my knee.

I'd laughed out loud when he appeared out of nowhere a few minutes ago and leapt on my leg with a squawked "Hello!"

Before I'd gone to read Stan yet *another* bedtime story (*anything* to help make him sleepy), the bird had been happily strolling up and down the still-damp papier maché crocodile that was basking on some newspaper in front of the TV. But I guess crocodiles – especially papier maché ones – can't scratch the top of your head when you're in the mood for it.

"Wow – I think this place needs a bit of a tidy-up," says Alice B. Lovely, surveying the room.

"Nah, it's OK," I say.

Alice B. Lovely shoots me an incredulous look –

and then we both burst out laughing.

I mean, the place is *trashed*.

There's the bowl (and random dollops) of leftover gungey paste from making the papier maché for the wonky wire-framed crocodile, never mind the endless tatters of sticky newspaper.

And while we'd been waiting for tea to be ready (fish fingers, noodles and beans), Alice B. Lovely got us all making monsters out of the floppy, ready-for-the-bin vegetables she found in the fridge (like I've said, Mum really hasn't been great with ordinary stuff like shopping lately).

Now there are a fine selection of only-slightly-mouldy veggie monsters sprawled out on the coffee table, with bodies made out of potatoes or avocado, and legs and arms of spring onions and carrots, held together with cocktail sticks. Alice B. Lovely awarded first prize to Stan, for his monster with an onion for a head, bits of broccoli for ears and mushrooms and raisins for "menacing" eyes.

They all look great (and of course Alice B. Lovely has taken photos of them), but we haven't *quite* got around to clearing away the chopping boards and the odds and ends of veggie scraps. A lot of which Buddy had helpfully cached, which we can see from the bumps here and there under the rug.

"Listen, I'm sorry Buddy ruined your book," says Alice B. Lovely, nodding down towards the vampire novel that was pretty much stripped of paper when we came back from our art tour. All that was left was the cover and a floor-full of torn and clawed pages.

(Some of the pages have been recycled into Stan's homework project croc, while the others – the ones under chairs and tables – I haven't bothered gathering up yet.)

"It doesn't matter. I didn't like it much. And neither did Buddy, by the looks of it!" I laugh.

"Yes, but I'll still buy you another copy," offers Alice B. Lovely.

"Please don't," I tell her. "I've gone right off the author. . ."

"Why?" asks Alice B. Lovely, blinking her silhouette lashes at me.

"She's a big, fat phoney," I say, jerking a little as I speak and disturbing Buddy. He flutters his wings and hops on to the arm of the sofa.

"Why? What's she done?"

"She came to my school for Book Week and did this talk," I say with a shrug. "She came out with this really dumb line, about how '*your dreams will come true, if you just believe in them. . .*' I just think that's so lame."

Alice B. Lovely says nothing for a second. I turn around to face her and she is leaning her head on the back of the sofa, her curtains of glossy fair hair spilling over behind it.

"Dreaming is fun," she says in a soft, thoughtful voice, as she stares at the ceiling.

I don't know what she's acting so thoughtful about. It's pretty obvious what the problem with dreams is.

"Not if you dream about something that can never come true," I say with an edge of brittleness in my voice.

Now it's Alice B. Lovely's turn to face me.

"What happened with your mum and dad?" she asks simply.

She knows.

She knows I'm really talking about Stan's dream about our parents getting back together.

Her honey eyes are locked on mine. I worry that she might genuinely be able to see inside my brain.

'Cause then she might find out that it's sort of *my* dream too.

I've been rumbled. . .

"You know how people fall madly in love?" I sigh at last.

"Yes."

"Well, my parents sort of fizzled *out* of love. It had been happening for a long, long time. It just got worse when they both started new jobs."

I think back to that final argument, when they just couldn't stand one more second of being with each other. Dad had threatened for the millionth time to leave, and Mum said, "Fine! And take *this* with you!", which was when the Arsenal mug got chucked and Dad stopped just threatening and actually left.

Eight o'clock exactly, one Friday night; that's when he went. I remember because the clock of doom chimed the time, so we'd never forget it.

Which reminds me; I haven't heard it chime in *ages* . . . did something *snap* inside it when I knocked it over this morning?

"I know it doesn't feel like it, but it'll be all right," says Alice B. Lovely, bringing my thoughts crashing back to Mum and Dad. "I don't mean straightaway. But it will be all right."

In the soft light of the table lamp, she looks like some mythical fairy-tale creature, and I want her to look into my future and tell me *when* exactly I might feel happy ever again.

But there's another creature in the room – one that's standing on the back of the sofa and pecking at my *head*!

"Buddy, stop it! What's he *doing*?" I ask, laughing and at the same time trying to pull away from Buddy's prying beak.

"He likes you – he's trying to groom you," says Alice B. Lovely, reaching over to help. "Hold still, and I'll get him to stop. Oh, did you know you've got a big tangle of hair here?"

"Yeah," I mumble, as she gets hold of Buddy and gently sends him flapping off towards the papier maché crocodile. "I've got quite a few."

I pat the smoother top layer of my hair down self-consciously. The mats I keep hidden underneath could probably make a cosy nest for a hamster. And don't even get me *started* on the never-ending nits. I feel itchy now that Buddy's fussed with my hair. Wow, I have *got* to sort myself out.

"I've got some really intensive hair conditioner at home," says Alice B. Lovely. "I'll bring it next time and sort all your tangles out if you want."

Gulp.

She's being too nice, just when I've relaxed a bit, and that's a dangerous combination for me.

I look away from her and dig my nails into my hands, trying to will away the tears. I wish for the first time ever that I had a pair of those big alien lobster claws; they'd be bound to hurt more.

"Don't."

It's just one word, but Alice B. Lovely says it at the same time as she takes hold of my hands and uncurls my digging fingers.

Double gulp.

This feels a little bit weird.

Well, a *lot* weird.

I mean, it feels like Alice B. Lovely could maybe help sort out more than one type of tangle for me. (Is that possible?)

As I dare to glance back up at her, I realize something with a start: Stan was right.

Alice B. Lovely really *is* special.

And it isn't just her mad clothes and her weird doll face and fake eyes and her strange pet.

It's just . . . *her*.

Alice B. Lovely *isn't* a big fat phoney.

She wasn't sucking up to Mum and Dad when

she said she liked their work – she was just really interested.

She wasn't trying to get Stan to like her when she took her soft toy to meet his – she thought it might make him happy. Same with cooing at passing pigeons and liking his homework and playing Tickle Tag and bringing around Buddy.

Even something dumb like that waiter in the pizza place; she didn't tell him I didn't like cheese 'cause she was butting in for the sake of it – she thought it was important.

That *I* was important. . .

And it is SO amazing to know that there are people in the world – apart from me and Stan and Tash – who *aren't* BFPs. . .

"Can I tell you something, Edie?" says Alice B. Lovely, suddenly leaning in towards me and brushing my hair away from my face.

Oh, please.

Oh, no.

I can't stand it if she's even *more* lovely to me.

I might start crying so much that I don't know if I'll be able to stop.

"Did you realize you have a bit of broccoli stuck to your eyebrow?"

BOING!

No, that's not the sound of the clock in the hall, which will never chime again, I don't think, 'cause I'm pretty sure the mechanism broke (oops) in the happy second it hit the floor.

Nope; that *BOING!* from somewhere deep inside me marks the moment my life switches from drab and dull to new and shiny.

It marks the *twelfth* time I have burst out laughing today.

(Oh, yes, I'm so sad – or so surprised? – that I counted.)

Twelve times; that's more than I've laughed in . . . well, since I can remember.

As Alice B. Lovely smiles at me and her startling eyes twinkle, I know I don't have to ask her when I will be happy again.

'Cause (*tick-tock, tick-tock*) with the two hands of my imaginary happiness clock perfectly placed on twelve, the answer is: *right now*.

And in case you can't guess, that feels pretty lovely to me. . .

Chapter 12

Just an (Extra)ordinary Day

It's just an ordinary Monday lunch-time.

Whatever's on the menu smells delicious, but I'm not hungry. 'Cause I'm full up with happiness, high on life and buzzing with a brilliant idea.

I've told Tash about the unexpected dollop of happiness I've been hit with, and she's well chuffed for me.

I've told her how after this weekend, life suddenly seems lighter, things seem brighter, and she slapped me a high five.

I've told her about the dumb stickers on the bus shelters and the broken clock of doom and the upcoming gum art show and the full-sized crocodile in the living room and she giggled out loud (bad – we were in chemistry at the time).

I haven't told her about the brilliant idea

buzzing in my head because it's only just occurred to me.

"Hey, why don't you come to mine after school? We could take Max for a walk, or just hang out in my garden," Tash suggests, as we hover in the long queue for lunch.

I hesitate.

Before Mum and Dad broke up, I loved spending after-school time with Tash, just 'cause she was my best friend.

After Mum and Dad broke up, I was *desperate* to spend after-school time with Tash, just 'cause it meant I didn't have to be around one crummy nanny or other.

Last week, I could've happily moved into Tash's, just so I didn't have to spend a nanosecond with Alice B. Lovely.

How funny to think that I'm now trying to figure out how I can let Tash down gently!

The thing is, I seriously want to head out of after-school club today and see the fabulous parakeet waiting for me in the huddle of drab starlings.

I couldn't care less if Dionne, Cara or Holly see Alice B. Lovely waving to me. In fact, I want to wave to her *first*.

Actually, I won't just wave; this afternoon I am going to shout out her name, so *everyone* knows she's my friend.

My *friend*, not my nanny.

(Alice B. Friend.)

"I don't know . . . I sort of promised to help Stan finish painting his crocodile," I say lamely.

At the same time, I am staring two people ahead of us in the queue.

And the two people happen to be Dionne and Holly. (Minus Cara.)

Dionne is standing chatting in a bored, couldn't-care-less way with Holly, her hands locked behind her head, her patterned alien lobster claws in full view.

And that's what I'm fixing on.

I take my phone out of my pocket, select the camera option, and hold it up.

"What are you doing?" asks Tash.

"Art," I say simply, zooming in on the alien lobster claws, in all their splendour.

This is my brilliant idea: just like Alice B. Lovely does her bus-stop installations, I'm going to photograph phoniness. Well, fakeness, anyway.

I've got Saturday's photo of Alice B. Lovely's lovely but non-real eyes and eyelashes.

Right now I can snap Dionne's painted and pimped nails.

Then there's that girl Jada someone-or-other in Year Ten who's had really obvious hair extensions, AND Mr Powell, the drama teacher, who's had his teeth whitened so much you need shades when he yells, "Come on, people, let's *do* this!"

CLICK!

Yep, this is the start of a whole new project for me.

"Hey!"

I hear the first hey, but don't assume straightaway that it's aimed at me.

"HEY!"

OK, so now I'm hearing loud and clear.

"What are you doing? Are you taking a photo of my friend?"

It's Cara, emerged from somewhere or other, come to join her mates and freaking out 'cause I'm taking a picture.

"*No!*" I lie, and feel Tash nudge me in the ribs with her elbow.

I guess my best friend is saying "What *is* she like?" in her own, coded way.

"Dionne! *Dionne!*" Cara calls out. "*She's* taking photos of you!"

Dionne whirls around, spots Cara pointing one of her own alien lobster claws at me, then steps away from the queue.

She comes and confronts me, followed – of course – by Holly.

"*Are* you? Taking photos of me, I mean?" she asks me to my face.

I wish some of the teachers who love Dionne and her buddies could see this now. Where's all the simpering and sweetness she turns on when I see her talking to them in the corridors or the playground?

"*No*," I lie again. "Why would I take a picture of *you*? You're not *that* interesting!"

I nearly "ooof" as Tash thumps me in the ribs again.

Huh? Why's she doing that?

"What's with your attitude?" says Holly.

"What's with *yours*?" I bite back, my anger reaching boiling point.

(Somewhere, the hands of my imaginary happiness clock are both still pointing to twelve. But the longer one is now juddering uncertainly.)

"Edie!" Tash is hissing at me.

I ignore her.

"What's your name?" Cara asks Tash, out of the blue.

"Natasha," says Tash, sounding nervous.

"Leave her out of this," I snap.

"A word of advice, Natasha," says Cara. "I've seen you around; you seem nice. Not like your friend. I'd ditch her and her lame attitude if I was you."

"Well, thanks for your opinion," I hiss at the high-and-mighty sixth former. "We're fine without it!"

(With a clunk, the long hand of the happiness clock takes a tick *backwards*.)

Cara, Holly and Dionne do what looks like synchronized eye-rolling and go back to the place in the queue that Dionne and Holly were in originally.

"Morons. . ." I mumble blackly, and look to Tash for a nod and an "Uh-*huh*".

But Tash isn't nodding.

She's not "Uh-huh"ing.

She's got her arms folded, her lips pursed, and is turned away from me.

Little Miss Sunshine seems to have a storm cloud hovering over her.

"What?" I ask.

"*Why*," she says, her lips tight but her voice wobbling, "do you *always* want to start a fight with everyone, Edie?"

What?

I do *not* want to start a fight with everyone!

And to show that what Tash has said is one hundred per cent not true, I say nothing.

I just walk away.

And wait for her to follow me with an apology.

Which she doesn't do.

I can't believe this . . . it just proves that – gulp – she sides with the BFPs more than me. And so I guess that makes my best friend a phoney.

How tragic is *that?*

So much for happiness. . . I think I just tripped into a big pit of *gloom*.

It's just an ordinary Monday, late afternoon.

Pigeons and seagulls are circling around us, mildly curious as to what a teenage schoolgirl with scraggly hair, her kid brother in an oversized blazer, a freaky person in vintage clothes and a pet carrier covered in a black cloth might be doing up quite so high in their sky.

And yes, I do mean *their* sky.

We are twenty-one stories up, not just staring out of a high-rise window but standing on the flat roof of this towering multi-storey block of flats.

It's like I found that mountain I was looking for,

where I can shout my worries to the wind. . . Only I'm too busy being amazed to think of anything but "Wow!"

"Not too close to the edge, Stan," Alice B. Lovely calls out, as Stan swoops and flaps, blissed out and thrilled to be up so near to the clouds.

There is a waist-high wall all around, but I guess she's just being super-careful, like a responsible nanny should be. Especially with all the exuberant running and swooping Stan's doing.

"Yeah, Stan," I copy her. "Just stay in the middle, OK?"

"You too, Edie. Don't forget I'm meant to be looking after you as well!"

Alice B. Lovely is gently teasing me, but I know she does care.

She truly *does* care, or she wouldn't have brought me – and Stanley – up here.

("It's just a blip. A little blip. We can fix that," she'd said, when I came out of after-school club, tensed-up and scowling, my head thumping with the effort of ignoring Tash and the upset of her ignoring me back.)

And what are we doing up here near the clouds, exactly?

To be honest (properly honest), I'm not sure,

'cause Alice B. Lovely said I just had to follow her and she'd show me something special.

"Isn't it beautiful?" says Alice B. Lovely, glancing around at the rolling hills in the distance, the ramble of rooftops and church spires reaching out to them, the sway of treetops in the park below.

Yes, the view *is* beautiful. Yes, it's incredible to be up here, in this secret, off-limits space. Did Alice B. Lovely think it would take my mind off my happiness blip? She might be right. . .

"So which is *your* house?" asks Stan, as he lollops past us in his flapping blazer.

He's not talking to me, obviously, since both our homes – Mum's flat and Dad's – are on the other side of the park from here.

"Down there," answers Alice B. Lovely, pointing vaguely at the streets of Edwardian houses stretching all around.

I might be all fired up with the stuff that's happened today – and waiting to find out why exactly Alice B. Lovely has brought us here – but I'm suddenly very aware that I don't know very much about her life. I spent so much of last week trying to pretend that Alice B. Lovely didn't exist that I ignored the fact that I was curious about her.

There are a whole heap of "Tell me something else?"s that I want to ask her. And straightforward questions; I have *lots* of those. Like. . .

- Which school does she go to? (Is she the coolest girl there?)
- Does she have brothers and sisters? (Are they as arty as she is, and their Auntie Maggie?)
- What does the "B" in her name stand for? (Brilliant? Beautiful? Bonkers?)

"Does you dad work in *that* park?" I ask, starting with a particular question that's just pinged into my head, and pointing down to the treetops.

Her dad's a park ranger; I remember *that* much. He once went on safari. She told Stan that when he was talking about Uncle Bob and how he ended up with Arthur (and I ended up with that useless, dumb *hippo*).

"Yes, that park, and other places," she says vaguely.

I don't mind about the vagueness.

I'd be vague if I had to describe *my* dad's job. "He designs websites . . . for a bunch of people."

"What about your mum? What does *she* do?" I find myself asking.

How weird. For the last few hours I've been seething, my head a mush of anger and embarrassment and betrayal. It must be the air up here; the wind from the faraway hills and the unseen sea beyond it are blowing the bad mood from my mind.

(The hands of the happiness clock are back exactly where they should be.)

"She works in fashion, a bit like *your* mum," says Alice B. Lovely, blinking today's eyelashes – the rainbow ones – at the birds circling all around us. "But just part time. She does other stuff too."

"Is that where you get your ideas about clothes?" I ask, intrigued.

My mum goes to work in her boring navy suit. I bet Alice B. Lovely's wears amazing things: 1960s Chanel-style suits, 1970s kaftans, 1990s rave neons, maybe. Who knows? I'm just about to ask when Stan comes swooping between us.

"*How* did you say you knew the code to get up here?"

His freckly nose is all crinkled up as he squints in the sunlight and I notice a brown streak of crocodile-coloured paint in his hair.

I also notice that he's a different boy from the one I've been hanging out with for the last few months.

That boy was pale and serious and clung on to my hand at all times. He lost himself in Lego for hours and had long, quiet conversations in his bed with his toy crocodile, telling him all about his nightmares. He hid behind me when we passed Mrs Kosma's pigeons, as they strutted under her windowsill, waiting to be fed. The only thing that got him even *slightly* perky was watching me torturing nannies.

But *this* boy in front of me is lightly tanned and grinning, happy to skip and run and swoop without any help from me. His Lego has stayed in its tub and Arthur gets thrown into the air and does a variety of somersaults at bedtime. He stood and chatted with Mrs Kosma at her window this morning before school, telling her all about Buddy as the pigeons cooed around his feet. And the only time he *isn't* extremely perky is when he finally falls asleep, and dreams his sweet dreams.

It's as if Alice B. Lovely somehow fixed him.

And Mum seems fixed too . . . she presented her amended designs at her conference on Saturday and no one could speak. She thought at first it was because her colleagues all hated the splashes of silver and blasts of cherry, but they were simply stunned into silence by the new design styles. They *loved* them. She loved that they loved them. She spent yesterday wearing jeans and bright colours and screaming her head off as we all got soaked on the rapids ride at the amusement park she treated us to, then got as messy as me and Stan painting his metre-long croc project.

And of course, I felt like I'd been fixed too, or at least had a plaster or two stuck on the painful bits.

All Saturday, all Sunday, all this morning, I'd walked taller, felt happier, laughed more, and sensed the gloom slip away.

Till lunch time. . .

"I told you already, Stan," Alice B. Lovely smiles at my brother, as she holds down her bottle-green velvet skirt, which is flittering and flapping in the breeze just now. "I used to visit someone who lived here. I know the codes to get in."

"Oh yeah!" nods Stan, happy with her explanation. "Can I feed my leftover packed lunch to Buddy?"

For a brief, windswept moment, I drift away, thinking how impressed I am at Alice B. Lovely's incredible memory. Not only does she remember the main entrance-door code to get into the building, but the code to this private, special place too.

"Well, yes, if you like," I hear Alice B. Lovely telling my brother, bending down to lift the black cloth a little on the pet carrier. She uses it whenever she transports Buddy around, she says. It keeps him calm and unstressed. "Don't lift the cloth too high, Stan, or he'll see the other birds and might get a bit anxious."

"So he doesn't ever have contact with other birds?" I ask, forgetting my small access-code question and remembering that Buddy lives indoors.

"Well, he watches them from the little aviary Dad built for him on our balcony," explains Alice B. Lovely, glancing up at me through her rainbow fringing. "He's fine there, when he can hop and fly from perch to perch. I guess he's at home enough not to feel threatened when he sees sparrows and pigeons and crows spiralling around."

I glance at the Edwardian terraces below and try to imagine Alice B. Lovely's house.

In my mind I see a first-floor balcony overlooking a glass conservatory, perhaps, and a gently overgrown cottage garden, stuffed with blooms and blossoms and heavily laden fruit trees.

I see a happy mum and dad at a huge dining-room table, laughing at the antics of Buddy and praising their daughter for her creativity when she shows them her latest images on her phone.

Maybe her dad has a study, full of bookshelves about wildlife, with framed photos on the walls from his days on safari. (My dad's always dreamed of having a study, instead of having a small workstation in the hallway.)

Maybe her mum's got a room too, with walls covered in inspirational odds and ends: clipped-out pages from magazines, strips of gorgeous fabrics. (Mum's always wanted her own space at home, instead of just plonking her laptop on the small kitchen table.)

And what's Alice B. Lovely's room like, I wonder?

Maybe she'll invite me and Stan around one day and I'll see for myself.

Maybe—

"Stan!" Alice B. Lovely exclaims as my brother opens his lunch box and a bunch of pretty random stuff tumbles out. "Why didn't you eat your dinner?"

"It was a bit horrible..." he says, holding up a sandwich bag with a dry-looking bun in it. The small bunch of grapes seems a bit sad and shrivelled too, and the best-before date on that yoghurt pot is long gone.

"What was in here?" asks Alice B. Lovely, holding the sandwich bag aloft as if it's a piece of evidence.

"Marmalade," says Stan, pulling a yuck-face. "Mum was busy getting ready for work, so I said I'd get my own sandwich. But there wasn't any ham. Or cheese. Or peanut butter. Or even jam."

"Right," says Alice B. Lovely, getting to her feet and rummaging about in her bag.

Is she going to get her phone and call Mum to tell her off? Or get in touch with Dad to let him know that Mum's failing in her parental duties? Or contact the Social Services? (Would they pay us a visit if they knew Stan was eating stale marmalade sandwiches and we didn't have any nit shampoo?)

"She can't help it – her brain's been a bit scrambled since she got her new job and split up with Dad," I say hurriedly, suddenly protective of Mum and her current domestic uselessness.

"Yes, I know," says Alice B. Lovely, producing not a phone, but a notebook and a pen. "I'm going to write her a long list of groceries and stuff. Then when we get back, I'm going to get on the computer and set her up with an account for online supermarket shopping. I'll get her to order it tonight."

"Or we could order it *ourselves* – I know her credit card number," I suggest.

"Good! And I'll book a delivery slot for tomorrow evening, when she's back from work. What time will she finish?"

"I'm not sure," I mutter, with an uncertain shrug.

On Tuesdays, Mum works extra late, since me and Stan are at Dad's. Who knows what time she'd finally fall exhausted through the front door?

"Fine. We'll worry about that later," says Alice B. Lovely, flicking the notebook open. "So what do we need?"

"Bread that's not rock hard for a start," I say, pulling a face at the sight of Stan struggling to pull a piece off his bun to feed to Buddy.

It makes me glad that I have school dinners.

Not that I had any today; I spent lunch time hidden round the back of the gym, sulking by the bins.

Argh, I'm in danger of thinking about Tash again . . . of setting the hands of the happiness clock juddering backwards once more.

I try to block her from my mind by chanting out my shopping wish list.

"Pasta – the twirly sort; jam – strawberry; tuna –

in brine; shower gel – any kind; nit shampoo – extra-stength. . ."

Alice B. Lovely scribbles frantically, pausing only to flick the breeze-swirled curtains of hair back from her face.

I amble around the open roof space as I talk, my mind jumping from the useful to the necessary to the delicious.

And then I walk around the big block shape that I think is the top of the lift shaft and see something kind of surprising on the far concrete wall.

A flutter of heart-shaped yellow Post-it notes.

There are maybe ten, stuck up here and there, in no particular pattern.

Some are a faded-by-sunlight lemon-white; some are bright crocus-yellow new.

They all have words on them, messages written in the swirly writing that I recognize from Alice B. Lovely's ad on the library noticeboard.

I lean closer.

Let them understand, says one.

Can things change, please? says another.

My eyes flick to some others.

Bring me luck!

Will it get easier?

Make it stop.

"Make it stop"? What's *that* abou—

"You found my worry wall, then!" Alice B. Lovely says brightly, appearing by my side. "It's what I wanted to show you, Edie. If things are bugging me, I come up here, have a think about what my problem is, then write it down and stick it up here."

"Does it really help?" I say dubiously.

"Yes, it does," she smiles, her sea-green eyes looking particularly vivid in the sunlight. "I feel like I've left whatever worry I have behind when I go back down to the ground. And I like the way the wind eventually whisks them away."

As if to prove the point, an extra strong gust chooses this second to loosen one of the faded Post-its – *Will it happen*? – and send it quivering and dancing into the sky.

Laughing, I watch as it then judders and tumbles through the air, heading off in the direction of the faraway treetops of the park.

"Maybe it'll land in a magpie's nest," I murmur.

"Maybe it will," says Alice B. Lovely, handing me a small Post-it pad and pen. "*Your* turn."

Alice B. Lovely leaves me alone and goes back to Stan.

So what will I write?

Maybe just: *Can we ever be friends again?*

Yep, that's it.

I take my time, doing my neatest handwriting, then adding swirls like Alice B. Lovely's for luck.

And then I stick it on the worry wall, give it a pat for luck, and walk away.

"Hey, how long before I get an answer to my question?" I call out with a grin to Alice B. Lovely, who's sitting with her back to me, beside Stan, Buddy's box and our school bags.

"Who knows? Maybe sooner than you think," says Alice B. Lovely, turning to look at me with a sparkle in her sea-green eyes – and a wink for Stan.

Stan winks back (with *both* eyes; he's not so great at it).

They seem to have a secret, but I don't mind.

I don't mind anything any more, even happiness blips.

'Cause with Alice B. Lovely looking out for me, I'm sure everything really will turn out all right.

In a weird and wonderful way, I bet. . .

It's an ordinary Monday afternoon at home.

I guess I should say *nearly* at home.

Somehow we've ended up having juice and biscuits in Mrs Kosma's flat – even Buddy, who's busy caching chunks of digestive under either his best friend Arthur the crocodile or one of Mrs Kosma's knitting patterns.

"Smile, sweetheart! Smile!" he squawks, happy in his work.

Mrs Kosma is beyond charmed.

"Oh, my!" she claps her hands.

Actually, I don't know if she's clapping her hands at Buddy's dexterous beak or the suggestion Alice B. Lovely has just made to her.

"He's just . . . *wonderful*," she exclaims, unbothered by the mess of crumbs Buddy is making. "And yes, of course I'll help you with the surprise!"

OK, so she was clapping her hands to both.

So why are we here, in a flat I've never once been inside before? (It's mostly made up of floral wallpaper and furniture, and several million framed photos of grandchildren I've never seen visit.)

And what's Alice B. Lovely's suggestion?

I think I'll answer the second question first: we'd been walking towards the flats, and spotted Mrs Kosma leaning out of her window, noseying as usual and feeding her fat pigeons.

"The shopping; why don't we ask Mrs Kosma to let the delivery guy in tomorrow, while your mum's at work?" said Alice B. Lovely. "Can you imagine the surprise of seeing all the bags?"

I had to think about it for a minute; would Mum *mind* having Mrs Kosma in the flat? But she was happy enough to have her come look after us last week (the night I set the pasta on fire), so I figured it would be fine.

The next question was, would Mrs Kosma be up for helping us with our shopping surprise?

"Excuse me," Alice B. Lovely had begun, as Mrs Kosma stared at her warily. "But me, Edie and Stan would like to arrange something nice for Mrs Henderson, and we wondered if you could help?"

Next thing we knew, we were being ushered inside and force-fed chocolate Hobnobs (which answers the first question).

"I won't just let the delivery man take the shopping upstairs, no, no," Mrs Kosma says now, shaking a fat finger at us. "I will put away all the shopping in the cupboards and fridge too!"

"Really, you don't have to do that!" I say, as I hand her my spare key. I feel bad now for thinking of her as nosey and wide and phoney. (Well, there's no getting away from the *wide* part, I guess. . .)

"No! It will be my pleasure!" Mrs Kosma positively beams. "Who else do I have to help around here?"

As she says that, I look at the photos on the wall again, lots of them taken outdoors in olive groves in baking sunshine. *Cyprus*, says the angular lettering next to a map on the wall. Is that where all her family are, I wonder? Is that why I've never seen these children in all the years we've lived here?

Is Mrs Kosma maybe a little lonely?

Did Alice B. Lovely guess that?

Has she just started to fix someone *else*?

"Thanks, Mrs Kosma," Alice B. Lovely says politely, and Mrs Kosma leans forward to pat her on her bottle-green velvet knee.

"Lovely girl!" Mrs Kosma smiles happily, without realizing she's got the lovely girl's name spot on.

Drrriiiiing! trills my phone.

"Excuse me," I say, as I slip my hand in my school bag.

Mrs Kosma goes back to admiring the cleverness of Buddy, who is now snuggling the soft toy crocodile which has just been pulled out of Stan's school bag.

I read my text message.

Sorry . . . can we talk?

Well, it looks like the worry wall and the yellow Post-it worked already.

I glance up and see Alice B. Lovely smiling at me.

She knows.

But before I get the chance to smile back, I realize something with a jolt of shock.

I forgot something.

Something really important.

There I was this afternoon, way, way up in the sky, and I completely forgot to be scared of heights. So much for this ordinary day; I think the girl with the rainbow eyes has cast some kind of spell on me. . .

Chapter 13

Hard Truths and Soft Centres

"Oof!" says a voice from somewhere down below.

"Uh-oh!" I wince. "I think I just hit someone!"

Me and Tash both hunker down out of sight on the balcony, bursting with barely contained giggles.

Yes, we're friends again.

Yes, she's here having tea with us at Dad's place.

Yes, I just clunked a man on the head with a piece of wholemeal bread that I was trying to throw to the ducks in the canal.

"Do you think he saw us?" Tash grins.

"Yes!" I grin back.

We're sitting like naughty six-year-olds who've just nicked some Jammie Dodgers out of the biscuit tin, clutching our knees and hee-hee-hee-ing.

It's like the moment in yesterday's lunch queue and the hurt and the happiness blip never happened.

Well, *sort* of.

I'm still a little battered and bruised from the chat me and Tash had on the phone yesterday afternoon, of course. Some of that stuff was hard to hear.

Though it took me quite a while to hear it, 'cause even after I'd got Tash's text and Alice B. Lovely said we'd have to make a move, Mrs Kosma had seemed determined to find ways to keep us all trapped in her living room. As we were gathering up our stuff (jackets and school bags and pet carriers) she was *still* trying to show us her wedding photos; the cosy cardies she'd knitted for her grandchildren in scorching Cyprus; the tiny sweet Greek pastries she loves ("Would the bird like to try a little baklava?").

But as soon as we escaped up to our flat, I left Alice B. Lovely to register with the online supermarket site, and Stan to play with Buddy, and shot into my bedroom.

Hunched on my duvet, I took a deep breath and called her.

"Tash, it's me," I said nervously, as soon as she answered her phone. "I got your text. Thanks."

"That's OK," Tash answered, sounding a little nervous herself.

(Weird. She seemed to be panting and snuffling.)

"Are you all right?" I asked, slightly freaked out.

"WOOF!"

"Sorry, Edie – *down*, Max! *Down!* Oh, don't lick my face right after you've eaten your tea! *Yeuch!!* Hold on . . . I'm going to put him outside my room."

There was more panting, some clunking, footsteps and a muffled "*Ha-wooOOoo*!"

I was pretty glad of the dumb dogness going on, to tell you the truth – it burst the balloon of awkwardness I think we both felt.

"Hi, I'm back!"

"Good. Great. Um. . ." I hadn't been sure what to say next.

Luckily, Tash had been thinking of quite a *lot* to say, so I mostly just listened.

Which was the painful bit.

"You were really angry with me today, weren't you?" she began.

"Well, *yeah.*"

"Did you think I was siding with Dionne and her friends?"

"Well, *yeah.*"

"I thought so, but I wasn't, y'know. Just 'cause I didn't side with *you*, doesn't mean I sided with *them*."

I frowned at the walls of my fearsomely yellow room, struggling to make sense of what she was saying.

"It's just that I got so mad at you, the way you always want to *argue*."

Me? I thought in shock. But I hated people who argued! It was number one in my "Things I Hate" Top Ten!

Wait a minute. She was talking about me never backing down, wasn't she? But hey, just 'cause I don't like to back down, it doesn't mean I'm actually *arguing* with someone. Right?

(Though, uh, I *guess* it could come across that way.)

"*And* you're always winding people up. It wasn't just Dionne and her mates yesterday. You do it to *everyone*. Even the teachers, sometimes. You've done it with every nanny as well. I mean, yeah, now and then the wind-ups can be a little bit funny –"

The time Wendi (nanny number whatever) fell for my '"hundred per cent true fact" about how keeping your mobile wrapped in cling film reduced the risk of radiation *was* pretty funny. It took about five phone calls with her shouting, "I CAN'T HEAR

YOU!! CAN YOU SPEAK UP?" for the truth to dawn.

"– but most of the time it just comes across as *mean*!"

Mean?

Me?

It was the most hurtful word that anyone could say to me, especially my best friend.

I couldn't speak for a second. Not because I was confused or shocked this time, but because the tears were rolling down my cheeks and I worried that if I tried to say anything in my defence, it would come out as hiccupped sobs.

"Edie?" Tash muttered my name.

I heard her, but my watery eyes were fixed on the bedroom door, which had opened ever so slightly.

A tiny head was peering round it.

No, it wasn't Stan, it was somebody, *something*, much smaller.

"Hello!" squawked Buddy, hopping through the gap and looking at me quizzically.

"Edie?" Tash repeated, as Buddy flap-flapped on to my knee and stared his beady eyes into mine, all the time tilting and dipping his head.

I stroked the smooth, shiny black feathers of his

neck and back and felt instantly soothed. Enough not to choke on my tears if I talked.

"But *I'm* not mean like Dionne and her mates!" I tried to defend myself. "Don't you remember that time when we started school? How they walked past us when somebody was asking what the 'P' stood for in my name? And one of them said 'Pathetic.'"

"Edie!" Tash said in surprise. "I can't believe you're still going on about that! I *told* you at the time, they heard someone say 'What does 'P' stand for?' and just made some stupid throwaway comment. They didn't *know* anyone was talking about your name."

"But. . ." I began, trying to think of a reply. Buddy nuzzled my fingers to carry on with their stroking.

"And face it, you've said and done a whole *bunch* of meaner things, Edie Henderson! What about the time you booed that Year-Seven boy when he parped all the wrong notes on his trumpet during assembly?"

But wasn't that just funny? Everyone had laughed.

"Or the time you told that poor student teacher Miss Kaye that she looked just like a model with her new haircut?"

Gulp. She'd looked more like *horse* with her new haircut, as everyone but poor Miss Kaye knew.

"Or last week, when you were so sarcastic to that author?"

Yeah, *maybe*.

"Or the way you've tricked and tortured every single nanny you've ever had?"

Guilty.

"And the dirty looks you're always shooting at Dionne, Cara and Holly . . . no wonder they're really wary of you!"

I froze then.

Did I really do that? But didn't they sneer at Alice B. Lovely and how she dressed? Though I suppose they didn't know I'd overheard. And I hadn't said very nice things about Alice B. Lovely's style to Tash. Never mind slagging off Dionne and co's alien lobster claws.

Suddenly, as sure as Buddy was a magpie, I knew I *was* a mean girl.

I was mean and sarcastic and spiky.

Had I *always* been mean and sarcastic and spiky, or had it just crept up on me?

It had become worse, I guess, as the arguing and the dark silences had happened at home. It's hard to be glittery inside when your life feels rough as sandpaper.

But was I stuck this way for ever?

Was I Edith P-for-Pathetic Henderson after all?

Miserably, I let the phone drop on to the duvet, half-heartedly pressing the speaker button on the way.

"Edie?" Tash's voice blasted out urgently as she listened to my silence. "Please . . . I'm not saying this to hurt you. I just – I just needed you to think about how you're coming across to people. I hate it when you're like that 'cause I *know* you're not deep down."

Actually, I'd been stuck in gloomsville for so long, I wasn't sure *I* knew what I was like deep down.

"Smile, sweetie! Smile!" squawked Buddy, breaking my mood.

"Ppfft!" I snorted out loud.

"Edie? What was that? Was that the *magpie* talking? Can you get him to do it *again*?"

"I don't know!" I laughed, as Buddy hopped and danced, delighted to see my reaction, I think.

"WOOF!"

"Oh, no . . . Max has just shoved his way back in. Hold o—"

"WOOF! WOOF! WOOF! *WOOF!!*" came Max's bark, loud and insistent.

"WOOF! WOOF! *WOOF!*" squawked Buddy.

Tears suddenly spilled down my cheeks, but not 'cause I was sad.

And I couldn't speak, but not 'cause I was angry, or hurt.

Alice B. Lovely and Stan, hearing the laughing (from me, and from Tash at the other end of the phone) and the woofing (a symphony of dog and bird) had come peeking in my room, to see what was going on.

We had a four-way, two-pet conversation after that, with Alice B. Lovely and Stan clambering on to the bed with me and Buddy, and all of us raiding the EMRGIZEE CHOCLIT supply.

And as we hung out there together, I realized that the pain of the truth was just part of my happiness blip.

The blip was over, and it was time to shake off the brittle shell I'd built around me. Time to show off my soft centre, as gooey and mushy as the chunk of caramel bar that I went on to find cached under my pillow in the morning.

(Who knew that soft centre was there? Alice B. Lovely, probably. . .)

*

"Edie! Why are you down there?" says Stan now, appearing at the doorway of the balcony.

"Hiding from someone who's not a duck," I tell him, grinning. "And what are you doing with a half a tree?"

Stan is holding a very large branch that is taller than him in his arms. Last I knew, he and Alice B. Lovely had gone out for a little walk, and it seems they've brought back a souvenir.

"We're making a perch for Buddy, for when he comes here to Dad's," he explains.

And last I knew of Buddy, he was in the bathroom, happily washing and preening in the inch of cold bathwater Stan had run for him.

"Where's the perch going?" asks Tash.

"Beside my bed. We're going to fasten it from the edge of the top bunk to the curtain rail."

"Stan, that's *my* bed you're talking about!" I pointed out. "*I'm* in the top bunk." (Sadly.)

"You don't mind swapping, do you, Edie?" says Alice B. Lovely, stepping out on to the balcony holding an iron and some thick fabric.

No, I do not mind swapping. After standing at the top of the world (or at least the multi-storey block on the other side of the park) I'm not scared of heights any more. But I'd be glad to have the bottom bunk, since there's more room, and less chance of me walloping my forehead against the ceiling on a twice-weekly basis.

"Nope, that's fine!" I say with a shrug. "Hey, listen, are you planning on trying to *iron* the branch to the curtain rail? 'Cause I'm no perch expert, but I'm not sure that's going to work."

Yeah, I realize that's *still* a little sarcastic, I know, but I figure if I go gently, with a smile on my face, then that's all right.

"I just found this material at home, and some tape that sticks fabric together with heat," explains Alice B. Lovely. "I'm going to attach it to the curtains in your room, since they're pretty thin. They must let in *so* much light. I don't know how you guys sleep!"

A lot better since *you* came along, I think, looking up at my fairy godmother, who just happens to be a sixteen-year-old beautiful freak with violet eyes and peacock-coloured lashes (today).

Tick-tock, tick-tock goes my happiness clock.

(It doesn't get better than this.)

"Oh, by the way, Edie," says Alice B. Lovely, spotlighting me in her gaze. "You know the gum art show that's happening at the art gallery this weekend?"

"Your aunt's show? Yeah, of course," I say.

"Uh, yes. My aunt's," she says, nearly dropping the heavy iron there, as she swaps hands. "Well, I've got two tickets for the preview evening, tomorrow. Do you want to come with me?"

(Wow, it *does* get better!)

"Yes, yes, of course!" I babble. "What time? Is it a sort of party? What do I wear? Do you have to dress up or—"

"DAAAAAAD!" yells Stan, hearing the lock turn in the door from his vantage point.

"Hi, Stan my man!" I hear Dad holler back, as I scrabble to my feet. "Look who *I* found downstairs!"

Mildly curious, we're all in the kitchen now, me, Alice B. Lovely, Tash, Stan and his giant branch.

"Oh!" laughs Mum, stepping into the room, followed by Dad. "I wasn't expecting such a welcoming committee!"

"Mum!" sighs Stan, throwing himself and his branch into a happy hug with her.

She's wearing her usual navy jacket, but with a big silver rose pinned on the lapel, and she's matched it up with her jeans. She looks like a smart version of her laid-back old self, instead of a stiff stranger in a suit.

"What are you doing here, Mum?" I ask, scratching my head with confusion. (And very possibly nits.)

"Well, I just *had* to come and thank you very, *very* much for the *lovely* surprise I had when I arrived home tonight!"

The shopping delivery. I'd completely forgotten about it.

"I know you had a bit of help from Alice and Mrs Kosma, but . . . well, thank you, my darlings."

Mum holds out an arm, so I can join the group hug alongside Stan and the branch.

"Don't we have lovely children?" says Mum, turning to smile at Dad.

"Yep, we certainly do!" Dad smiles back, leaning comfortably against the door frame.

My parents.

The soon-to-be-divorced Mr and Mrs Henderson have just smiled at each other.

It really doesn't get better than this.

And I know who's behind this minor miracle.

Alice B. Lovely, I might just love you. . .

Chapter 14

Having a Ball

There were three steps leading up to the art gallery entrance.

Tap, tip, tap!!

My best black ballet pumps followed in the footsteps of Alice B. Lovely's antique gold shoes.

A smallish queue of people are ahead of us, waiting to file into the exhibition.

"Good evening, sir. Straight on through, please."

"Good evening, madam. Here for the preview?"

"Good –"

The man taking tickets in the foyer must have seen plenty of strange and unusual sights here in the art gallery.

They're just usually on the walls, I suppose, not standing right in front of him.

"– evening, girls," he manages to say with the

merest of surprised pauses, then immediately regains his composure. "The show is in the main hall, and the cloakroom is on the left."

No wonder he lost his professional cool just there; Alice B. Lovely has really outdone herself tonight.

After taking care of me (nit shampoo, intensive conditioner, tangles slowly-and-sometimes-painfully untangled, faint hint of glitter on my cheekbones) she'd disappeared into the bathroom looking like her usual crazily retro self and returned as a swan.

A staggeringly gorgeous vintage swan *princess*.

"Whoooahhh!" Stan gasped, holding up Arthur for a better look. (Arthur was lonely tonight . . . Alice B. Lovely left Buddy at home, since we were going out.)

"Do you like it?" Alice B. Lovely asked sweetly. Twinkling diamanté stickers – same as the ones on her library Post-it note – winged out gracefully from the outer corners of her eyes.

"You look *astounding*, Alice!" Mum said, as she plonked her big work bag on the sofa beside me. "Where did you get that dress?"

"It's an old petticoat, actually," says Alice B. Lovely. "Victorian, I think. It's just something I found in a jumble sale. That's where I get most of my clothes."

The petticoat hung like a sleeveless white shift dress, with a delicate piece of lace edging the bottom of it. Her tights were white with silvery sparkles, mismatched with her old favourite gold shoes. Over her shoulders was draped a white, silky fringed shawl, hanging as straight and shimmering as her long fair hair.

But it was her eyes, her Snow-Queen eyes, that you couldn't stop looking at.

"It's like they're covered in *ice*!" Stan had said, breathless with wonder, as he came for a closer look at her frost-tipped white lashes.

"They go beautifully with your contact lenses!" said Mum admiringly.

Alice B. Lovely was gazing at us all today with the palest-of-pale blue eyes, the piercing colour of a husky's.

"You have quite a collection of eye fashion, don't you?" Mum smiled. "Are they very expensive to buy?"

"Not really; I order them over the internet. There are lots of sites that sell them," Alice B. Lovely answered, hugging a mesmerized Stan to her. "I just save up my evening babysitting money – and now what I earn from *this* job – to pay for them."

"How do you fix them on?" asked Stan.

"Glue. Well, just for the eyelashes, not the contacts," she explained, with one of her harp-in-the-room gentle laughs.

It was funny, even though she'd happily revealed the secrets of her fairy-tale look, it still didn't take away from the fact that she was like something out of a storybook.

And here I was with her at the art gallery now, in my skinny grey jeans, matching top and cardie and Gap hoodie. It was as if I was a mouseling that had been transformed into Cinderella's human servant on the night of the ball.

"What's a cloakroom again?" I check with Alice B. Lovely, recalling what the guy on the door had just said.

"Where you can leave your coats and bags," she says, as she glides along the wide shiny corridor.

"So is that what we should do?" I check, wriggling out of my fleecy hoodie.

Alice B. Lovely almost trips up in mid-glide.

"Uh, no ... you don't *have* to put your stuff in there," she says, sounding distracted, as if something has ruffled her swan feathers.

Right. I guess she is only wearing the shawl and

carrying the tiniest old lady pearly handbag in the crook of her arm.

My hoodie feels pretty hot in here, actually, but I can just carry it. (Yes, I admit I'm too shy to go to the cloakroom on my own.)

"Are you OK?" I check with her.

Alice B. Lovely is tip-tapping along towards the main exhibition room again, but seems to be blinking her frost-framed eyes an awful lot.

"Yes, I'm good. It's going to be amazing, seeing this show before anyone else, isn't it?"

"Definitely," I nod.

For a second I think about asking her how she got the tickets, but by now I assume she can do just about anything. She has almost magical powers.

Powers that make cross parents happy; sad boys glad; gloomy girls laugh; locked doors open to the sky.

Still, the answer is obviously much less exciting . . . she got them from her Aunt Maggie, of course.

"Look, Edie!"

We're in a crowded, brightly-lit room filled with chatting and smiles, funky music and waiters swooshing around with trays laden with drinks and food.

It feels very grown-up. I feel nervously excited.

"Everyone who's here," I mutter, glancing around, "who are they? Are they famous?"

"No! They're just ordinary people who like art, who've become members of the gallery. And if you're a member, you get invited to previews like this."

Her eyes aren't on the milling men and women, though; they're on the huge blow-up photos on the wall. All those tiny works of gum art, suddenly magnified to at least fifty times their true size. If they were fantastic when they were small and secretive, they're truly gobsmacking large and unmissable.

"Where's your aunt?" I ask as we bumble along, bumping into other admiring onlookers as we study the images.

"She'll be somewhere here," Alice B. Lovely murmurs, distracted by the pictures. "But she'll have to chat to lots of people, so I said I wouldn't bother her. I'll catch up with her some other time."

"Right," I nodded, my gaze drifting from one amazing blow-up to another.

A roaring motorbike, fire coming out of its exhaust.

William and Kate.

A bunch of balloons.

Super Mario.

Hello Kitty.

A squirrel.

A rainbow.

A jar of jellybeans.

An angel.

A kid doing cartwheels.

An old-fashioned double-decker bus, and lots more besides.

The images are funny and clever and cute.

Especially – in my opinion – THIS particular one. . .

"Look! *'Countdown to happiness'*!!" I practically squeal, pointing at the clock I saw on the pavement outside the charity shop. "Here – here's my phone. Can you take a photo of me beside it?"

I don't care any more whether this clock matches the imaginary one in my head. I don't care if it's just some dumb coincidence. I just know I love it.

"Of course!" giggles Alice B. Lovely, delighted to see how excited I am to be here, to see and share this stuff with her.

And as the camera on my mobile clicks and the flash fades, I realize quite how much all this matters to her.

"You'd *love* to have an exhibition like this one day,

wouldn't you?" I say to Alice B. Lovely as she hands me my phone back.

"Definitely," she says with a wistful sigh.

"I can just see all your bus-stop photos here!" I say encouragingly.

"Yes, but I want to do *more* than those," she replies, turning her ice-blue beam on me. "I've got this crazy dream of decorating a bus shelter! I'd get lots of stuff from jumble sales: cushions for the plastic bench, net curtains to hang up, maybe get a rug down on the pavement—"

"And how about a little table, with a vase of fake flowers in it?" I suggest, inspired by the wall-to-wall florals of Mrs Kosma's living room.

I wonder if I could ask Mum to lend me the clock of doom to put on the table too. Its chimes are well and truly broken (Mum took it to the jeweller to see if it could be repaired, but the answer was thankfully "no"), though it still tick-tocks in the middle of the night like someone's playing a glockenspiel in the hall. Maybe it won't sound so loud in the great outdoors?

Or maybe I could get especially lucky and someone might steal it?

"Yes! A table and flowers would be *so* cute," Alice B. Lovely laughs her delight, reaching an arm around my back for a pleased squeeze, and dipping her head down on my shoulder closest to her. "You really get it, don't you, Edie?"

She whispers those last few words, and I think of the yellow fluttering Post-its and their peculiar messages. (*Let them understand* pings into my mind.)

"Excuse me?" someone interrupts us. "But is that *you* over there?"

Alice B. Lovely lifts her head and we both look at a young guy who is pointing over to the other side of the huge room, the side we haven't reached yet.

As the crowds part for a second, we see a wide-eyed face gazing back at us, with the name "Alice B. Lovely" encircling it.

"Yes," my friend answers, of *course*, her cheeks pinking ever-so-slightly in her ivory-pale face.

"I thought so!" says the guy. "Listen, I work for the local newspaper. Can I interview you about being an artist's muse?"

"Hey, tell him you're her niece!" I mumble in the direction of Alice B. Lovely's tumble of silken hair.

"What's that?" smiles the reporter guy.

"Uh, it's, um, nothing," says Alice B. Lovely, blushing a little more pinkly.

You know, she is *so* amazingly unshowy. Other

people would be acting all phoney, yelping out loud about how they were connected to someone even just a *tiny* bit famous. But not her; not Alice B. Lovely.

"Right. Well, could I maybe steal you away, anyway, for a chat? Over by your portrait?"

Alice B. Lovely gives a startled but happy shrug, her curtain of hair rippling and her silky shawl slipping off one shoulder.

She might look like the swan princess, but I'm suddenly feeling like an overcooked jacket potato, and I think I might look like one too. It's getting really, really busy and stuffy in here, and right this second, I'm not really wanted.

"You go on," I tell her. "I'll catch up with you when you're done!"

I'm suddenly, thankfully not shy any more, just sweaty. And while Alice B. Lovely gets "interviewed" by the newspaper bloke, I'm going to go leave my bulky hoodie in the cloakroom after all.

I head out of the packed, chit-chatting space into the cool marble corridor and follow the signs for where I need to be.

Not sure what to expect, I'm pleasantly surprised to walk into a small area with a smiley lady at a counter, a book of raffle tickets in her hand and a rail semi-filled with coats and jackets behind her.

"Can I help you, my love?" she says breezily.

I relax. Everyone at the show is quite trendy in their own way, but this lady – Norma Grimley, it says on her name badge – is as unfashionably ordinary as any of the mumsy, friendly dinner ladies at school, which makes me feel instantly as ease.

"Could I get this hung up, please?" I ask, placing my hoodie on the counter.

"Anything else, sweetie?" says the lady, selecting a raffle ticket from her book.

I instantly break into a grin.

She almost sounded like Buddy, there, with his "Smile, sweetie! Smile!" line. How funny!

"Yes. I mean no," I correct myself, pulling off my grey cardie. "Can I put this in too?"

"Of course!" says the woman, taking it from me. "Having a nice time looking at all the funny pictures, are you, dear?"

"Um, yes," I answer, trying not to smirk. It didn't sound as if she was too impressed with the artwork. "I'm here with my friend. Her aunt did all the chewing gum paintings."

"Really?" says the lady, raising her pencilled-in

eyebrows as she slips my hoodie on a hanger and places it on the counter, ready to ticket. "Not really my cup of tea, I have to say. A bit . . . *silly* for my taste."

I have an instant image in my head of Alice B. Lovely explaining her bus-stop art installation idea to Norma Grimley and nearly choke on my giggles.

"Right, that's one done," says the cloakroom lady all efficiently, going on to pick up my cardie. "Oh!"

"Oh!"?

What could be "oh!" about my plain little H&M cardigan?

The woman seems to have spotted something on it.

She picks the something off, and for just a moment there – seeing the arcing white shape – I think it's a feather from Buddy's white chest.

"Is this Ali's?" she says.

"What?" I say back.

"Is she here, dear? Did she come?"

I'm completely muddled and befuddled. I have no idea what – or who – Norma Grimley's on about.

Tip-tap-tip-tap-tip-tap!

It's a tiny delicate noise, but I'd recognize it anywhere.

Tip-tap-tip-tap-tip-tap!

Out there in the hall, Alice B. Lovely is running.

Running from what, exactly?

Dring!

"Excuse me – I have to go!" I babble at top speed, wrestling my hoodie off the hanger before charging out of the cloakroom while attempting to answer the phone I can now hear trilling urgently in my handbag.

Dring!

This is madness, I think, fiddling with the reluctant catch on my bag.

Dring!

If I was in the mood for daydreaming (and wasn't suddenly spooked), I'd think my ringtone was like the clock in the old fairy tale, striking twelve as Cinderella ran from the ball.

Dring!

Perhaps there's a chance I might *just* get out of here and find one of Alice B. Lovely's gold shoes on the steps of the art gallery, being held up by the young reporter guy.

Dring!

"Miss? Here, miss, don't forget this!" the cloakroom lady calls out to me, holding up my grey cardie in one hand.

Dring!

"Thank you!" I say, quickly doubling back and taking it, while finally managing to fumble my bag open.

Dring!

Good; I've got the phone in my hand now, but it's hard to press the right button at the same time as running.

Dring!

As I hurtle out into the corridor and head for the main entrance and frantically press "answer", I feel the cool evening breeze on my face.

Dring!

The chill stills me.

Dring!

And I can see mumsie Norma Grimley freeze-framed in my mind, the millisecond after I gratefully snatched my cardigan from her.

Dring!

The thing she's still holding in her other hand; it's not a white feather.

It's an eyelash.

Dring!

"Hello? Hello? Where are you?" I say into the mouthpiece, glancing around for a sign, any sign, of Alice B. Lovely.

But it's too late, I've missed the call. . .

Chapter 15

When the Clock Strikes. . .

"Let me see. . ."

We haven't had a second together so far this morning; every time I tried to talk to her, to show her the message, something irritating (like our French teacher) got in the way.

"Here," I say, handing my phone over to Tash.

We're on the wall by the sixth-form block. It's quiet and chilled compared to the main playground area, which is full of flying footballs, shrieking girls and roaring boys at break time.

So, SO sorry, Edie!! I felt really terrible. Just HAD to get out of there. . . Let me know you got home all right? A xxx

"And did you text back?" asks Tash, passing me the mobile back.

"Yeah, about a million times," I tell her. "I kept

saying it was fine, and asking where she was, and what was wrong. Then I texted her again when I got to Mum's, to let her know I was there. And I texted her again and again and again, but she never replied."

"What did your Mum say?" asks Tash. "She must have freaked out at your coming home all on your own!"

Secrets and lies . . . they're not a great combination.

But I didn't feel there was much else I could do, or I'd get Alice B. Lovely into terrible trouble.

"I told Mum she'd left me at the front door," I admit to Tash. "I said that she'd waited till the door locked behind me and waved me night-night as I went up the stairs."

"Oh, Edie!" says Tash, nibbling at her lip.

Uh-oh. She can't put one of her positive spins on this.

This is serious.

"But what about today after school?" Tash frets. "Is she picking you and Stan up as normal, or. . ."

That "or. . ." hangs in the air.

The longer neither of us says anything, the bigger the "or" gets, like an ever-expanding bubble that's about to—

PROD!

A sharp nail is in my back.

I turn round and see it is attached to a finger that is in turn attached to Cara Connelly.

Great.

She's about to pull sixth-former rank and tell me and Tash to get back to our part of the school, isn't she?

But instead of giving me a hard time, Cara's passing me her phone.

Huh?

"This is your mate, isn't it?" she says. "Dionne said I should show it to you."

I'm looking at something that seems to be from the local newspaper's website.

The headline says, "Art At Your Feet!" – with a photo of a woman with red, curly hair crouched down, dressed in a grubby boiler-suit and painting gum on the pavement. The caption says it's Maggie Baxter, and the feature beside it is a review of the show at the gallery.

"Go further down," Cara says, probably spotting my confused frown.

I scroll, and there; *there*, underneath the review, is the blow-up photo of Alice B. Lovely's painted, fluttery-eyed face, with the real Alice B. Lovely standing beside it.

A smaller headline reads: "Who's That Girl?"

My eyes quickly scan what comes next.

Mystery surrounds a girl claiming to be the niece of local artist Maggie Baxter. Our reporter tried to talk to the girl, known as Alice D. Lovely –

"It's Alice *B.* Lovely!" I find myself raging, though it might as well have been "D", since I've never found out what the "B" stands for.

"Shh!" Tash hushes me, already skimming ahead in her reading.

– who appeared in an outlandish outfit at last night's private viewing.

Outlandish?! I bristle. Alice B. Lovely looked like the most beautiful, fantastical, *special* person in the entire room.

When interviewed about her likeness, the girl seemed happy. But the moment our interviewer spotted Ms Baxter and tried to get "niece" and "aunt" together, the teenage girl bolted. Ms Baxter was later quoted as saying she was no relation; the girl was simply someone she'd spotted on the high street one day, coming out of a charity shop. She seemed so unusual that the artist felt compelled to paint her. She had no idea how the girl had managed to get tickets for the exclusive preview show.

I keep opening and shutting my mouth, unsure

what to say.

Luckily, Tash and Cara don't seem to expect me to say anything.

"Here," says Cara, using her index finger with its long, alien lobster claw to scroll down a little further.

And what she's scrolled to is an embedded video, very probably shot by the "nice" young reporter guy.

It shows Alice B. Lovely looking into the lens, a hunted, panicked look on her face, and then she turns and runs, becoming a fuzzy blur of white as she disappears along the marble-tiled corridor. She's heading for the open main doors and the enveloping black evening sky beyond.

"Have you got to this last bit?" says Holly, wandering over with Dionne.

Another set of alien lobster claws hold out a mobile that they want me to look at.

If you know this girl, please call, email or tweet us on...

It's on the tip of my suddenly poisonous tongue to spin around and say, "What? So you want me to get in touch and tell them whatever I can?!"

But before I slip back into my bad old ways, to a time before I felt happy, I realize that no one – not Cara or Holly or Dionne – expects me to do that.

They're simply showing it to me as it is.

"Hey, check it out," I hear Tash say. She has her own (normal) finger on the screen of Holly's phone and she's scrolling to something that's caught her attention.

I hold my hand over the screen so I can see it easier in the sunlight.

It's a Twitter thread.

This girl go 2 my skool: Mary Magdalen Girls High. Fact. Her name Ali sumfin. She in 6th Form. She well crazy. Fact. LOL

I'm cold and hot and cold and hot and cold again.

The hands of the happiness clock are trembling, *straining* to spring backwards.

"You OK?" says Cara, digging her alien lobster claws into my shoulder.

Ali.

I've heard that name before.

But the very end of last night seemed like such a blur I'd forgotten about it till now.

"Yeah, I'm OK," I say with a non-committal nod. I don't feel *remotely* OK, but even if Cara and her friends aren't as bad and horribly obnoxious as I used to think, they're still not people I trust to share my innermost thoughts with.

I save that for the trusted few: Tash, Stan, Alice B. Lovely . . . and maybe Buddy.

But since Alice B. Lovely has gone AWOL, I guess that just leaves the girl, the kid and the magpie.

"What are you thinking?" asks Tash, who, like I say, knows me way, way, *way* too well.

She's frowning.

I think she might be guessing that I'm about to do something I shouldn't.

"I've got a really bad headache, and I need to go home," I lie, as I get up and walk off. "Can you let the teachers know?"

"Edie! EDIE!!" she calls after me, but I'm not looking back. . .

Mary Magdalene High School for Girls is on the other side of the park from my school.

According to its website . . .

- the school motto is: "Every Girl Counts" (pretty lame; why not extend it to "Every Girl Counts And Is Quite Good At English Comprehension Too"?)
- start time is a very early eight-thirty (ouch)
- home time is an equally early three p.m. (nice)

*

I guess that early finish time is the reason Alice B. Lovely could offer her after-school nannying services; most other schools in town don't get out till three-thirty. And with me and Stan in after-school clubs, Alice would have *tons* of time to wander home and transfer Buddy to his pet carrier before turning up outside our school gates.

But today it's *my* turn.

I thought Mary Magdalene High School for Girls would be some dramatic-looking Victorian turreted pile, but it's a dull and doomy modern block. I pictured the gates being huge and gnarly swirls of iron, but they're institute-plain bars. Actually, the place reminds me more of a prison than the Harry Potter-esque castle I had in my head.

I don't know why exactly I imagined it that way. I suppose I thought that it would suit Alice B. Lovely more. *This* place and Alice B. Lovely go together like haddock and ice-cream sprinkles.

Tick-tock, tick-tock...

It's nearly three.

I'm not standing right up close to the grim gates with the waiting mums and dads and childminders. I've chosen a spot further along, with a bush for cover.

I've seen a lot of greenery since I walked out of school, mainly because I've spent most of that time in the park.

For who knows how long, I sat on a bench and stared at the photo Alice B. Lovely took of me in the gallery, stupidly happy and full of hope beside the *Countdown to happiness* clock.

Then I walked and walked myself in circles, trying to understand what's happened, to think of reasons why the newspaper got it all wrong.

To figure out why Maggie Baxter might have said that Alice B. Lovely *wasn't* her niece.

To guess why Alice B. Lovely ran out of the gallery, and ran out on *me*.

But instead of figuring anything out, my mind has spiralled into a tangled muddle, repeating the same few sentences over and over again. . .

What really happened last night?

Did that reporter tell the truth?

Or has there just been some dumb mistake?

But then why did Alice B. Lovely vanish?

And when I haven't been slouched on a bench or stumbling around, I've been lying flat on my back on the grass, staring up at the towering tower block, wishing I could be up on the flat roof once again.

Up there in the cool, pure breeze I could gaze down at the swaying green treetops full of nests, or up at the close-to-the-touch clouds and circling birds and fluttering Post-it notes.

As I lay on the damp ground, I visualized a yellow heart-shaped Post-it in my hand, with my message written on it: *Is Alice B. Lovely just another phoney nobody?*

Help; that thought is shoving it's way into my mind again and I've got to ignore it.

Alice B. Lovely is the *least* phoney person I have ever met.

She is *not*, and never *has* been, a BFP.

She is genuine, amazing and caring.

There *is* an explanation.

There *has* to be.

Which is why I'm here.

DRINNNNNNNNNGGGGGGG!!!!!

A bell blasts out, and almost instantaneously, hundreds of girls pour out of Mary Magdalene High School.

Hundreds of girls in the most horrible uniform: brown blazers; brown ties; brown pleated skirts worn down past the knees. It's like waves of mud are sluicing towards the gates. I worry for a second that I won't be able to spot her, but then I remember she's in sixth form; they often get to wear normal clothes. And even if she's forced to wear the drab and dreary uniform, there'll be no disguising the waterfall of hair, the freaky doll eyes.

I stare and stare.

Girls come and go.

The sea of mud slowly tapers off to a trickle.

All I see is an older girl or two making their way out, followed by a bunch of young-looking Year Seven types, snickering and giggling together. There's virtually no one waiting at the gate any more.

The next person I'll see will probably be the caretaker, come to lock up.

Where *is* she?

Didn't she come to school today?

I should have asked her the name of her street. I could've gone round to her house now, knocked on her door, found out the truth.

Instead, I've skived off, and will have to face my fearsome form teacher tomorrow for nothing. I should've thought about this more. I should've—

Uh-oh. The Year Sevens, they've just barged into one of the older girls, and are laughing.

The older girl, mousey-looking with a brown

hairband, rights herself, but says nothing.

"Out of the way, grim girl!" one of the younger ones bellows.

"Grim girl, grim girl, grim girl!" the others chant as they go running and giggling ahead, through the gates and off down the street.

I don't know what the name-calling's all about, but I do know a bunch of nasty girls when I see one.

The older girl in the headband comes out of the gate and stares after them.

When she does this, her back is to me, and I see that her fair hair is tied into a long, loose plait that courses down the back of her dull brown blazer.

With a lurch of shock, I know.

It's her.

It's Alice B. Lovely.

She's moving off now, crossing the road, and I follow her with jelly legs and a thumping heart.

Into the park we go, my eyes glued to the clumpy sensible black loafers just ahead of me.

What am I going to do? What am I going to say? I've had hours to think of possible questions but they've all fizzled and popped out of my head. But seeing this girl I think of as a parakeet, a vintage doll, a swan princess disguised as a shy, plain schoolgirl has thrown me.

It makes my head swirl to think she goes home every day and transforms herself from this moth-coloured person to the butterfly that turns up and waits for us.

But why does she do something so extreme?

And where's she going now?

She's slowing down. . .

She's stopped to talk to a street cleaner guy who's emptying a bin by a park bench.

What's she saying to him?

Asking him the time, maybe?

If she's planning on picking up Stan as usual, she'll have to get going on her extreme makeover.

The thought of Stan fans a flame in me. If she *is* some kind of fake – a BFP like all the others – then she *can't* be trusted with my gorgeous little brother!

I stride over, while a scream boils inside me.

She suddenly sees me coming and her pale face turns ashen, her invisibly light eyelashes fluttering in panic.

The man in the yellow reflective jacket and thick rubber gloves clanks the emptied bin back into place.

"Everything all right, love?" he asks, glancing first at me, and then staring at a silent and stunned Alice

B. Lovely. "Ali? C'mon, smile, sweetie! Smile! And tell me what's going on!!"

My scream is stifled with shock.

There's a badge on his fluoro jacket. It's got the council's emblem on there; his name and job title, in bold letters.

STEVE GRIMLEY: REFUSE OPERATIVE

I'm not any kind of genius, but I have a hunch that he might know a woman called Norma Grimley.

And that they might have a daughter called Ali.

Who has a horrible nickname of "Grim Girl" at her school.

Wouldn't it be funny if I just opened my mouth and said, "Ali Grimley, pleased to meet you!"

But instead, I think I might just join the cross-country team at school.

'Cause all I do these days is run, and run, and run.

"Edie!" I faintly hear her calling after me.

But I'm gone, reaching and fumbling in my pocket as I stumble, my fingers frantically searching out my mobile so I can delete the photo that . . . that *whatever*-her-name-is took of me last night at the gallery beside the so-called happiness *gum* clock.

Tick-tock, tick-tock.

STOP.

Chapter 16

Tell Me Something True

A plate piled with baklava is sitting on a flowery doily, which in turn is sitting on the highly polished coffee table in front of us, along with two tall glasses of milk.

Stan is slowly chewing on a piece.

He's been slowly chewing on it for quite a while now.

The baklava's absolutely delicious, made of honey and nuts, but it might as well be made of papier maché for all he's enjoying it.

"Edith, *darling*," pleads Mrs Kosma, standing small and wide in front of me. She has her pudgy hands held palms together in front of today's black dress, as if she is praying.

"No," I say firmly.

"*Pleash*, Edie," Stan begs me, through a mouth full of sweet pastry.

"You don't understand," I tell him.

How *can* he understand? He's only six. I'm thirteen and *I* don't understand.

One minute, life according to Edith P. Henderson is gloomy and complicated.

The next it's bright, light and beautiful.

But now hands of the happiness clock are giddily spinning, *whizzing*, backwards out of control, and here I am, dumped into that familiar world of gloom and complication – with added, extra disappointment, just for fun.

"But the lovely girl! She is *very* upset, and *very* sorry," says Mrs Kosma, who's been back and forth to her open bedroom window, having conversations with Alice B. Lovely before returning to the living room to relay them to me. "Can't you just listen to her?"

"*No.*" I repeat again. "She's a liar. Why would I want to listen to any more of her lies?"

I don't mean to be rude to Mrs Kosma. I didn't even mean to get her involved. After I left (OK, ran away from) Alice B. Lovely or whoever she is, I went straight to Stan's primary and pulled him out of after-school club.

I'd planned to head for home and let ourselves

into the flat, but then I remembered Mrs Kosma still had my spare key, from sorting out the supermarket delivery the other evening.

So I'd ended up ringing her doorbell.

The minute she saw us standing there – well, saw me *crying*, I suppose – Mrs Kosma insisted we come inside.

And that's why we're here in her flowery flat.

Outside her flowery flat right now, probably surrounded by cooing pigeons, is Alice B. Lovely, who's come to apologize or explain or tell me some more phoney stories. I don't know.

With a sad sort of sigh, Mrs Kosma pads off. I hear chat.

She comes padding back.

"The girl said for me to give you this, Edith, my love."

Mrs Kosma hands me a yellow heart-shaped Post-it note.

It has one word on it, in her swirly writing.

Please?

Stan leans over and reads it out loud, after finally gulping his Greek treat down.

I look at my adorable, freckle-nosed brother . . . and decide to do it for him.

Furious as I am, maybe I can get answers. Enough, at least, so I can tell Stan why Alice B. Lovely can't be our nanny any more when he asks.

"Let me do this on my own," I tell him, as he goes to follow me off the sofa.

Stan looks crushed. But hey, don't we *all* feel that way?

Taking a deep breath, I head towards Mrs Kosma's bedroom, and the window she uses to watch the world go by, feed her birds and hold unsuccessful peace talks with a girl I can't trust.

"Edith, darling," says Mrs Kosma, bustling behind me. "Not in there. I tell Alice to come inside the main entrance hall; her magpie was getting upset at the pigeons so close around its box."

Mrs Kosma is motioning to the front door of her flat. Then she backs away into the living room, to give me some privacy and keep Stan company, I suppose.

And I suppose she is expecting me to open the front door – but I'm not going to.

Instead I creep silently up to it and squint through the peephole. It's still a bit of a shock to see the pale, ordinary girl in the brown hairband and dull uniform. Stan wouldn't recognize her, I bet, if she wasn't carrying the black-covered bird box.

"Hello!" squawks Buddy, and makes me jump away from my spying spot.

("Smile, sweetie! Smile!" the guy in the park had said. So no guesses where Buddy picked it up from.)

"Edie? Please can I talk to you?"

My heart's pounding. I say nothing for a few seconds, till I can be sure my voice is able to carry words without them wobbling.

"OK," I say curtly. "But like *this*. I'm not opening the door. I don't want to look at you."

"All right. . ." a sad-sounding voice answers from the entrance hall of the flats.

I'm hit by a sudden wave of exhaustion and let myself sink down to Mrs Kosma's patterned carpet, my back against the white-painted door.

I feel a little thump from the other side and realize she must've done the same.

"Honestly, I didn't mean to hurt you, Edie," she begins. "I just wanted you to be happy!"

You know, I don't really want to hear that. The rage in my head won't let me listen. I just want plain facts. So I start with an obvious question.

"Who are you?"

"I'm . . . I'm Ali Grimley. *Alice* Grimley," she says, stuttering slightly.

I knew that much already, of course, but I needed her to admit it.

"Why did you change your name?"

"It's 'cause... Look, I don't like being *me* very much. Being me is hard, sometimes."

I gulp. There have been times over the last few months, since Mum and Dad split up, that I haven't liked being me much either. But this isn't *about* me, it's about *her*, this lying, phoney stranger.

I want to know more, but with my scrambled brain I'm not sure what questions to ask.

Then I remember the game she played with Stan, that first day we knew her.

"Tell me something else," I demand, trying to force my voice to sound stern.

"Um . . . I guess I don't get on with many people. Well, *anyone* at school, really. They all think I'm weird. Even the *teachers*."

The Post-it notes on the worry wall . . . some of the scribbled messages are starting to make sense now.

"Tell me something else," I demand, as my mind whirls.

"My parents – they don't get me either. I mean, I love them and they love me, but I think they're just totally confused by me and the way I dress, and the stuff I like and the art I'm into."

Oh. So perhaps some of the yellow heart-shaped messages were to do with them as well.

"Tell me something else," I say, pushing on.

"OK . . . uh . . . well, out of school, I love dressing up – it makes me feel like a different person. The person I'm *really* like inside; the me who likes art and vintage clothes and getting people thinking; not the me who gets called 'Grim Girl' at school. So, I decided to give myself a different name too."

Suddenly I feel the tiniest twang of sympathy.

There were times in the last few months when *I'd* have liked to be a different person.

But then again, not to the extent that I'd openly *lie* to people, like *she* did.

"Tell me something else," I say, hardening my voice.

"I played around with lots of ideas, but I came up with Alice B. Lovely, just 'cause – 'cause I think I imagined it looking really *great* on an art gallery wall one day!"

As I press my back into the door, trying to get closer to hear her better, I notice the living room door opening.

Stan and Arthur; they're sneaking out, tiptoeing towards me.

I think about shooing them away, but instead I put my finger to my lips, so my brother – and his crocodile – know to be quiet.

"Tell me something else."

"She's not my aunt. Maggie Gibson. I mean, of *course* I'd love, *love*, LOVE to be related to someone like that – it was such a buzz when she offered to paint me that day! – but I'm not."

Stan stares at the door, listening, then sits down and snuggles beside me, nuzzling Arthur into my arms.

"Tell me something else," I say more softly, knowing the fire has gone out of my voice.

I hear a deep intake of breath through the few inches of wood separating us

"I live with Mum and Dad in the block of flats we went to. They're the caretakers of the place. It's only a part-time job, so Dad works as a street cleaner too. He loves being out in the fresh air, specially in the park. He found Buddy there, when he was just a tiny fledgling. Remember I told you about that?"

Stan looks up at me imploringly, and makes Arthur nod his soft, squidgy head.

"Tell me something else," I say, ignoring her question. So much for her father being some kind of posh-sounding park ranger.

"I told you my dad went on safari when he was younger . . . but it wasn't in Africa. It was in Great Yarmouth. He worked at a fun-fair ride called The Safari when he was a teenager."

Stan silently slaps Arthur's paw to his knitted mouth, to show how shocked he is.

"Tell me something else."

"And I told you Mum works in fashion, like *your* mum. I said that because I really *wanted* it to be true. And it is, sort of . . . she's the cloakroom attendant at the art gallery. She's the reason I got the tickets to the preview show."

I'd sussed *that* part out, at least, I think to myself, as I give Stan's shoulders a comforting squeeze.

The shock of it all is settling into just a shade of weary sadness for me now. I'm glad I deleted that photo on my phone; the *Countdown to happiness!* clock is nothing but a doodle on a spat-out chunk of gum, nothing more.

But I can't help asking the same question again, in case there are any last pieces of the puzzle to fit in.

"Tell me—"

"WOOF! WOOF!! WOOF!!!!"

Outside somewhere there's the panicked fluttering of wings and urgent cooing of distressed birds.

Mrs Kosma – always alert to her bird friends – hears it and comes hurrying out of the living room as fast as her creaky knees will take her and disappers into the bedroom.

"Oh, my! That naughty dog!" she calls out, obviously looking out of the open window.

I scramble to my feet, same as Stan, and hurry to the bedroom as well. I'm sure I recognize that bark. . .

"Sorry! Sorry!!" Tash is calling out, as I see her chase Max around the grass with the lead and the collar he's obviously slipped out of.

I'm guessing she's come round to check on me, since I dodged out of school, and probably because I've been dodging her calls and texts all day too.

She's not the only one checking up on me; Dad's car has just pulled up!

"Edith, I call your mum and dad when you first arrive," says Mrs Kosma. "I was worried about you and not sure what was happening!"

When she went to get us the baklava and the glasses of milk from the kitchen, she must have phoned them then. . .

CLUNK!!

That was the sound of Mrs Kosma's front door shutting.

SQUEEEE!! Thud.

And that was the main entrance door beyond that opening and thumping closed.

I hadn't even realized Stan had left my side, but there he is, running past the girl in the brown school uniform standing on the path, and he's jumping into Dad's arms.

"WOOF! WOOOFF!!!" barks Max, thrilled with seeing people he knows, especially people he knows running about like him.

He doesn't know *which* way to jump, so he pounces on the nearest person, who happens to be Alice B. Lovely.

"Max – get down!" yelps Tash. "GET DOWN!!"

Max's puppy training must be going well; he does what he's told and flops to the ground.

And finds his nose next to an interesting-smelling box.

"Edie!" Dad calls out, with Stan wrapped around him. "What's going on?"

What's going on?

Currently a couple of pretty terrible things, actually.

The first is that I have just spotted Mum stomping up the street, with a face that's a mixture of concern and fury. (I suddenly realize she may have had a call from school, as well as Mrs Kosma – it's policy for parents to be called if kids have unexplained absences.)

The second is that Max has started scrabbling at the door of the pet carrier, and before either Tash or Alice B. Lovely can stop him, he has managed to loosen the catch . . . and a petrified black and white bird hurtles into the air, swooping and squawking and flapping its wings so hard that several monochrome feathers flutter down.

"No!!" shrieks Alice B. Lovely. "*Nooooo!!!!*"

In the general scheme of things, yes, I might be angry with her, but right this instant, I'm frightened for Buddy.

He could fly off and be lost for ever!

He'd starve; he doesn't know how to find his own food.

There are hawks out there who'd be more than happy to swoop on a naïve magpie with no clue about the outside world. . .

"We've GOT to get him back down!" I call out to

anyone who might be able to help.

But we're all flapping around ourselves: me, Mrs Kosma, Alice B. Lovely, Tash, Dad, Stan.

"Justine! Thank God," Dad suddenly calls out, as Mum now speeds her way towards us. "*You* always know what to do. How can we get Buddy to come back?"

Mum stares up at the whirling bird for a second, then snaps out some orders.

"Tash, take Max inside now, and keep him quiet!"

Tash shoots a hand out to catch the keys Mum throws her, then throws herself at her dumb pup, scooping him up in her arms and letting herself into the entrance hall of the flats.

"Right, we need to get something that'll attract him down. Something he likes. Any ideas?"

I expect Alice B. Lovely to speak, but she's standing trembling, her eyes – her natural, dull-grey eyes – fixed on the traumatized bird up above.

"Maybe some bread? I get some bread!!" Mrs Kosma suggests, and scurries off to her flat.

But Stan has beaten her to it.

Before we even knew it he'd scrambled indoors, grabbed his school bag and is back, yanking Arthur out and holding him up.

Alice B. Lovely spots what he's doing and seems to snap out of the daze she's been lost in.

She holds her arms aloft, gives a whistle, then calls out, "Come on down! Come!! *Please*, come on down, Lulu!"

Lulu?

Lulu?!?

Does the *magpie* have two names, same as *her*?!

(Don't even get me *started* on the boy bird/girl bird thing. . .)

"It's working! Look! It's interested!" says Dad, as Buddy/Lulu makes ever-decreasing circles, spiralling lower and lower towards us.

"Hello!" laughs Stan, as the bird eventually lands with a thunk on his shoulder.

"Hello!" squawks Buddy/Lulu, as it nuzzles the toy croc that my brother is holding up to it.

I'm closest to both bird and boy, so I do some swooping of my own and gently grab the magpie.

Alice B. Lovely has already lifted up her pet carrier, and after I slip Buddy/Lulu inside, she fastens the catch with shaking fingers.

Our eyes meet.

"Lulu?!" is all I say.

"Yes," she nods. "It was just a spur-of-the-moment

thing. I just came out with Buddy, when I first took her here."

"But why?" I say with a weary shrug.

"Well, I – I knew it was one of Stan's nicknames," says Alice B. Lovely. "And I thought it might make Stan more likely to be interested and less nervous around Lulu. *Buddy*, I mean."

At that moment, Stan walks over and stops by my side.

With an earnest expression he looks up at Alice B. Lovely, studying her face.

"Who are you?" he asks simply.

Oh, wow.

My brother really *doesn't* recognize her.

Tears trickle from the small, dull-grey eyes of the ordinary girl in the brown uniform.

"Hello, Stan," she says in a soft and sorry voice. "My name is Ali. . ."

Chapter 17

Some Things That Don't Bug Me and One Thing I Love

Tick-tock, tick-tock, tick-tock.

That's the sound of the happiness clock, still going strong, a whole year on.

Oh, yes – it did and *does* exist. In my head and on my wall (I got the photo from the gallery blown up into a print). The original tiny one on the pavement has pretty much faded away, thanks to rain and constant footsteps.

As for the clock of doom, it clunks on, though now it's down in Mrs Kosma's flat, after she unwittingly admired it once and Mum practically *forced* it on her as a thank-you present for all the help she's given our family. (Who knew Mum lay awake in similarly long, sleepless nights listening to the dreaded drumming of minutes and hours dragging by?)

Of course there've been a few little blips along the way, but I try not to get hung up on those.

I try not to get hung up on *lots* of things that used to bug me.

Do you want a quick list, off the top of my head? All right; in no particular order, here goes. . .

- **False nails:** Hey, everyone is free to like what they like, even crazy fashions that make it difficult to text or squeeze your spots.
- **Heights:** Nana took me and Stan on the London Eye last Easter and I loved it, which is pretty amazing for me, since I'm someone whose head went woozy after three steps on the bunk-bed ladder not too long ago. (Though I *did* keep a yellow heart-shaped Post-it clutched in my hand during the whole ride which read, *Remember, this is OK!*)
- **Yellow:** It's fine. It's the colour of sunshine and heart-shaped Post-it notes, and it reminds me to stop moping if I'm sliding that way. I *have* stuck a couple of vampire-book posters up on my walls, though, which counterbalances the overpowering cheerfulness.

- **Soft toys on beds:** Don't laugh, but I now have a hippo called Maurice on mine. It's the one I got from my uncle who went to Kenya, remember? Stan said Arthur wanted him for company when we're at Dad's, so that's where he lives, on my bottom bunk. (I can never say no to Stan, after all.) I did think about customizing Maurice to stop him looking so cutesy, but then Buddy pecked his glass eyes out and did the job for me. She was a little jealous of Maurice and Arthur's friendship, if you ask me.

  (Yep, we stuck with calling her Buddy, 'cause Stan says she "likes it". And hey, it's a cool name for a girl, don't you think?)
- **Big Fat Phoneys:** Since all the stuff happened with Alice B. Lovely, it dawned on me that acting a little phoney – with the exception of some of our rotten ex-nannies – isn't *that* terrible.

  People might do it to be kind (like the author-who-I-won't-name, with Charlotte Adamson), or because they're lonely (Mrs Kosma, noseying at all the neighbours) or because they just want to be nice (Alice B.

Lovely, even when she took it too far, and found herself fibbing).

- **People arguing:** That's *their* problem. Maybe it's easy for me to be laid back about this now, since Mum and Dad don't do it any more. Honestly – *really and truly* honestly – they are nice and polite to each other these days, and even laugh at each other's jokes (!).

Get this: we all went out for a family meal on the day their divorce came through. Tash thought that was dead weird, but me and Stan were cool with it. The way we see it is, if you can't have parents who *love* each other, it's a good second best if they quite *like* each other. Which means, if you hadn't noticed, that last-minute number eleven on my original list of "Things I Hate" *definitely* doesn't bug me any more. 'Cause I *did* get what I wanted: parents who don't hate each other and a family that's vaguely happy. (I can live without the local, handy mountains, no problem.)

Oh, and before you go checking back, I have to say that Mum's choice in mushy rom coms still make me barf, nits haven't grown on me (except when they do, *literally*) and cheese is . . . well, all wrong. Stan tried to introduce me to the delights of stringy cheese, which is his current packed-lunch favourite, but he soon stopped when he spotted me giving it to Buddy, who ended up caching it in Stan's gym shoes. (Very unpleasantly squidgy when you're jumping on the trampet, apparently.)

By the way, Stan is still my assistant.

But not in torturing nannies.

Oh, no, those days are *long* gone.

In fact, we don't *have* nannies any more.

Mum and Dad each try and do a couple of super-early finishes in the week, so they can pick Stan up from school, while *I* make my own way home.

The rest of the time, Mrs Kosma fusses around us, making our tea, hand-feeding Stan baklava and knitting us truly terrible jumpers.

Mrs Kosma; I can safely say that she loves looking after us, and Buddy too, of course. As part of a pet-share, I mean, when Buddy's not living with me and Stan upstairs at Mum's, or staying over at Dad's.

"Finished!" says a voice now.

"What took you so long?!" I say, with my usual sarcasm.

I'm up a stepladder, taping net curtains to the side of the bus shelter. The cushions are already Blu-tacked in place on the red plastic bench. I've set up a little table too, with a flowery lace-edged square, lent by Mrs Kosma, with strict instructions to give it back once we've finished our art project.

"Do you like it?" says Stan.

My brother has added a bird cage to the table. He made it out of an old cardboard box. It has a tiny wire-and-papier-maché flamingo in it, perched on a squint branch.

"I *love* it!" I say, trying not to smirk. I look at my watch. It's six forty-five on Saturday morning, and it's going to start getting busy here soon.

Stan and I need to clear up and then take a few photos: first, we'll take one of the bus shelter as it is, and later, once it gets busy, we'll snap puzzled passengers.

We're going to email the pictures to Alice B. Lovely later, to show her that we believe in her dreams (*and* her), even if she's not around any more.

Where is she?

Has she flapped her fairy-tale wings and fluttered off?

Blinked her ice-storm eyes and magicked herself away?

No.

It's not *that* enchanted an ending.

Almost, but not quite.

The afternoon that Buddy was nearly lost . . . what happened?

Well, as we all shook and swayed, my mum took control.

Justine Henderson herded us all – kids, soon-to-be-ex-husband, dog, bird and nosey elderly neighbour – inside and up to her flat.

What followed was endless cups of tea, stony silences, bursts of chattering explanations, hugs and tears. *Lots* of tears. (From me, mostly, but who's counting?)

There was baklava too (brought up by Mrs Kosma, who felt those in shock needed sugar).

There was also open-mouthed staring (from Stan, who crept closer and closer to the strange grey-eyed girl, till he *finally* recognized her – despite her disguise of normality – and ended up resting his tufty-haired head in her lap).

"All the stuff you made up . . . did you just want to fool us?" I remember asking this different/familiar person, testing her *one* last time, as my hands ached to hold hers.

"No!" she'd cried, looking heartbreakingly sad and lost, her beautifully slate-coloured eyes misting over. "At first I did it 'cause I wanted the job. I wanted the money to buy things I was desperate for, like my clothes and art stuff and new contact lenses. And then. . ."

She didn't finish.

Not till I stared at her so hard she *had* to.

"I – I did it 'cause you and Stan, and your mum and dad . . . you all believed in me. The *real* me," she'd said, tears trickling down her pale cheeks. "And that felt *amazing*!"

At that second, there wasn't a sound – apart from Max quietly howling in the kitchen he'd been shut in – from anyone.

Me and Alice B. Lovely ('cause that's who she'd *always* be to me) grabbed hands, and with elbows bent, held them up in front of us like the hands of a clock, pointing to twelve. . .

A little while later, Dad drove her home and made Alice B. Lovely tell her startled parents just *how* unhappy she was at school. Thanks to Dad's advice, they pretty quickly let her switch to a sixth form specializing in art.

My parents are also helping her go through

various art school prospectuses so she can decide which one to apply to in the future.

The downside is that Alice B. Lovely is. . .

a) studying hard, and
b) a long way away.

She's going to a college – one where you *don't* have to dress in a mud-coloured uniform, and no one minds if you wear different coloured eyes and eyelashes every day – which is ten miles away, near her (100% real) Aunt Betty's, and so she's staying with *her* most of the time now.

I guess that's pretty much perfect, since Alice B. Lovely gets on great with the aunt she's named after. (Alice *Betty* Grimley! Who'd have guessed that's what the "B" stood for?)

CLICK!

I take a photo of the bus shelter in all its glory, then look at the image on the tiny screen – and laugh.

The whole thing is glowing, glimmers of light radiating, as if a magical presence has decided to perch its fairy-tale bum on one of the second-hand cushions.

I know it's just a trick of the early morning light, rays of slowly rising sun glinting against the clear plastic walls of the bus shelter.

But the wild-eyed Alice B. Lovely has made me see that there are sprinkles of specialness everywhere, if you just know where to look.

And I'm looking, all the time now.

Because the one thing I can honestly say I love is. . .

Life according to

Life according to...

Alice B. Lovely

Karen McCombie

SCHOLASTIC

First published in 2012 by Scholastic Children's Books
An imprint of Scholastic Ltd
Euston House, 24 Eversholt Street, London, NW1 1DB, UK
Registered office: Westfield Road, Southam, Warwickshire, CV47 0RA

This edition published in 2015 by Scholastic Children's Books

ISBN 978 1 4071 5848 8

A CIP catalogue record for this book is available
from the British Library.

Printed by CPI Group (UK) Ltd, Croydon, CR0 4YY
Papers used by Scholastic Children's Books are made
from wood grown in sustainable forests.

3 5 7 9 10 8 6 4 2

www.scholastic.co.uk